SHE FOUND LOVE
IN THE PROJECTS

AUTHORESS LEM

Mz. Lady P Presents, LLC

She Found Love in The Projects

Paris Narcole Lee

Since I was a little girl my mom talked to me about no-good men, but I never listened and that day had come to pass. Here I was losing myself behind a damn man that did nothing for me, but suck and fuck on me whenever he felt the need to. But I never complained because in my head, I was the only bitch he had. I was the only bitch he had been coming home to up until recently. But being naïve, I thought he was on the block getting it in. Silly of me to think that I would be exempt from fuck boy activities.

"Pussy bitch!" I screamed at my boyfriend of three years, and his side bitch, Cola. I didn't know the hoe real name and didn't care to speak on her. However, today was different, and I was pissed the fuck off.

"Come on, Paris, fuck them!"

"Don't fucking touch me! I lost everything behind this nigga. I refuse to allow this type of disrespect." I never meant to raise my voice at my best friend, Cassidy. She was just doing what any friend would do and technically, she was all I had in this crazy-ass world.

My story was different, I didn't grow up in the hood or poor, I was a good girl that loved a hood nigga. The day I chose to be with Gus was the day, I chose to live in the projects over the mini-mansion my parents raised me in. My father is King Malachi Lee; he was our Pablo Escobar. Because of his status alone people feared coming close to me, but not Gus, he didn't take no for an answer and that alone drew me to him.

But just like any other parent, my mother and father saw something in Gus that I hadn't seen. I was blind because he had given me a feeling I had never felt. He was my first everything, but I should've known that everything my parents had said would come back and bite me in the ass. However, I hadn't talked to them in three years, so I wasn't about to call now.

"You can be mad all you want, but I refuse to let you make an ass of yourself out here." Cassidy was right because all these hoes only worried about other people's business. But I was not about to give them a bigger show than I had already given them. I would walk away now, but this was far from over.

The elevator took forever to come, so I chose to wait today, instead of taking the stairs like I usually would. I was worn out from that little scene I had just caused. I felt as if fire was shooting through my veins; my heart was aching, and the feeling of emptiness was slowly creeping up on me.

It was crazy how hard I fought my parents to be with this man only for him to sell me nothing but dreams. I tried to be the girl that believed in her man, but I long ago faced the fact that he wasn't shit. I'm starting to believe I only stayed for the sex, then again, I don't know if it was even all that good. He wasn't my first, but I'ma just assume he was my best.

"You good, P?" The elevator ride was so quiet, I actually forgot Cassidy was on here with me. Just as I was about to open my mouth, we had reached the floor.

Taking a deep breath, I dropped down on my sofa and stared off in space. Life was crazy, and I was all out of tears; I wasn't even mad at Gus anymore. I was mad at myself for not seeing the signs that were right there. This time around, I had brought all this on myself; there were too many times where I had showed him a weak me. But he knew damn well, I was, indeed, a bad bitch.

I stood at 5'2," I had a caramel, blemish-free complexion, honey brown eyes, and plump lips. Bitches around here were paying for the waist and ass that I had at the age of twenty-six; I was damn near the baddest female in any hood. My waist-length, homegrown Remy just topped everything off.

"Paris, as your friend, you know I have to keep it hot with you. You are entirely too beautiful to even settle for the shit you've been settling for. Let that nigga go 'cause a dog only roam for so long before finding their way back home."

"Honestly, I don't think I want that nigga back. I'm confused as fuck about him and his girl in matching Gucci outfits, but he around here acting like he can't find work."

Just saying that shit had me reflecting on all his bullshit ass lies. Gus was no fairytale ass boyfriend, but I loved him through the struggle. I stood by his side, and I didn't want or need anything in return besides loyalty. I hadn't talked to my parents since I was twenty-three years old because I chose this fake ass love. But I guess this was my karma for disobeying my parents.

"Fuck, Gus, he's going to get what's coming for him. But enough of that, my cousin is having his welcome home party today. Come with me, it may help take your mind off the situation."

Rolling with Cassidy 'didn't sound like a bad idea. Its been forever since I had been out or even had a good time. Gus always had me sitting in the house, but I guess it was because he was living two different lives, and didn't want me seeing.

"I'll roll. Where is it, so I can know how to dress."

"Uptown, by my grandmother's house."

"Bitch, I'll be sure to grab Bella"," I said, referring to my gun. It was bad Cassidy's grandmother stayed in the Haynes Projects uptown. The worst projects in South Louisiana probably. I knew everybody would be out; it was summer, and typically that was everyone's hangout spot.

Cassidy and I talked for a little while longer before she left to go get dressed. Time was flying, and I was ready to go out and have a great night. It was time I drove the fucking boat that Meg talked about, instead of sitting on my ass on the side. It was summertime, and I was freshly single, and I knew for sure I wasn't going backwards this time around.

After showering and applying lotion to my body, I stood in the mirror and glanced over my perfectly naked body. I can't believe I got to a point where I was really insecure about the way I looked. There was a time, I didn't love myself enough, so I would rather have sex with my top on and bottoms off.

It was hot as hell outside, so I chose a pair of Adidas shorts, and a white tube top, and a pair of Yezzy's on my feet. I threw my hair in a messy bun and finished my look off with some lip gloss and a pair of diamond studs. Hearing Cassidy come in and scream my name, I did a once over in the mirror, grabbed Bella, and headed for the door.

Before I knew it, we were in uptown.

"Come on, bitch!" I got out, following behind Cassidy,

but not before turning my nose up at the bitches every-where, twerking.

"Thought you were on the hot girl shit." I looked at Cassidy and burst out laughing. I guess she caught the look that was plastered on my face.

We quickly grabbed a seat and started throwing back shots of D'usse. Chilling with my girl made me forget all about the drama that had happened earlier. It made me realize that I hadn't really lived much, but I was about to start living. I got up from where I was seated, and joined in on the twerking and hood rats' activities too.

Jarcole "Meech" Smith

"Damn, cuz, you can't speak"?" I walked up on my cousin, Cassidy, and her lil' homegirl, throwing back shots.

It had been five years since I last seen these projects, and I had to admit, I missed this shit. Even though the streets were what made me do a five-year bid. I missed this shit like a muthafucka, on God. But this time around, I would make sure not to go back in there. I made a promise to myself that they would have to take me dead.

I have been doing this street shit for so long that it was kind of all I knew. When I was ten, I moved in with my grandmother, Irene, my cousin Cassidy, and her brother, Nut. I guess my grandmother birthed some ain't shit ass kids because our parents did the same thing, left us to go chase a fucking high. My mother ended up dying, Cassidy's mother still came around, but shit, she ain't stop chasing that high yet.

By the age of fourteen, I was cooking dope for the neighborhood drug dealers and at sixteen, one of the biggest Kingpins in South Louisiana fronted me a brick, and put me on a block by myself. I stayed on that block from sunup to sundown until I came up off that brick. He took me under his wing, and I was up since then. Even at the age of twenty-eight, I can't be fucked with and that was a known fact. I left at twenty-three and still came back standing on a nigga's chest. Killing niggas and dealing drugs came to me with ease, but I wanted to chill out, and no longer wanted to stand on the blocks.

"I'm sorry, cuz. I saw you over there talking business and didn't want to interrupt you." Cassidy reached in and hugged me; I missed having conversations with her. When her brother Nut died, I became her protector; it really was just us, so I know how hard it was on her when I went away. She voiced it every day!

"This my friend, Paris; Paris this my cousin; Meech."

Shorty was indeed a bad one, but even through the smile she had plastered on her face, I could see that she had a story to tell. Had I been the same nigga, I was before I went to jail, I would have tried her out. But she was too pure, and any nigga could see that. I shook her hand and walked away to go holla at the rest of the people out there.

"Hey, daddy!" Tosha said as she walked up on me.

I had been ducking this crazy bitch all day. I really had nothing to say to her; she left a nigga high and dry when I was locked up. She wouldn't even let me call and talk to my daughter. I guess she thought I was about to sit longer than I was supposed to. I didn't trust the stupid bitch, and I definitely wasn't in the mood to be bothered with her today.

I was about to dismiss the bitch until I saw Cassidy's friend fighting some bitch. Shorty looked innocent, but she was handing the brawd she was fighting as if she grew up around niggas all her life.

"Paris!"

'The fuck this nigga doing out here?' I thought.

Shit was weird, but it wasn't my business, so I just turned back to continue finishing dogging Tosha's bald head ass out.

"Why the fuck you in my personal space?"

"Damn, Meech, you not going to forgive me? I told you I was scared and didn't want our daughter seeing you that way, baby." I gave her a knowing look because this was the same line every bitch spoke when it came down to a nigga going to jail. I ain't feel like hearing any more lies and after the shit, I was hearing about her, I would be sure to get Jordan tested. This hoe was out here moving like a snake all this time.

I walked off, leaving her standing there, looking stupid. It was my first day out, and I didn't want to be around any drama. Noticing Cassidy and her friend was straight, I continued walking passed them and straight into my grandmother's crib. I had to find out about shorty; it was something about her that had me wanting to know more.

"What up?" I said, speaking into my phone.

"Where the fuck you at, nigga?"

"In Mama crib; they got too much going on out there."

"Bet!" was all Jare said before he made his way in the crib.

Just like me, Jare had his own story, he had his parents, though. He was faced with a hard time when his mother went away to prison where she later died. He never met his father and from my understanding, his mother didn't care to speak on him. He chose the street life, instead of work-ing. He was two years younger than me, but I gave him the game, and he ain't turned back since. Jare was the defini-tion of loyalty and you rewarded loyalty with loyalty.

"What that pussy ass nigga Gus got going on out there"?"

"Man, I saw that shit and brought my ass in here. That

nigga too phony for me. The fuck you in the middle of the projects, rocking that fake ass Gucci. Then, got the nerve to match that hood rat ass hoe." I couldn't help but laugh at the sight of them when I first saw the two of them walk up.

To this day, I still think Gus was the one who put them bricks in the car I was in and had the people pull me over. The bitch had to see me one of these days, though. I might just let him think shit sweet for a while. He wanted to be down so bad, he probably would've set his own mama up to get on and the bitch still ain't on. He and King had business while King treated me like his son, and he made it very clear that no one is to do business with Gus. Niggas knew not to cross him, so they knew not to do business with Gus.

3

Paris

My fucking blood was at the point where it was boiling, you get caught cheating, but you put your hands on me in public. I was so fucking embarrassed, I jumped up and beat the fuck out of Cola, because I knew I couldn't beat Gus's ass. I was tearing the hoe up until I heard my father's voice from behind. His voice was so stern and cold it sent chills down my spine. Most girls would be happy to see their dad, but instead of running in his arms, I got up from where I was and walked away.

On the ride home, both me and Cassidy were quiet for the first time in my life; I had nothing left to say. I didn't even understand why the fuck my dad was out there, I knew my grandmother, Madea, stayed out that way, but why was he at the party? Pulling up to Terrebonne Projects, where I lived, I jumped out the car and ran for my place, I was so shame and hurt, I locked the door behind me and headed straight for the shower.

I wrapped a towel around me, and fell to my knees and began to pray.

Dear God,

It's me Paris Narcole Lee! I know it's been a minute since I came to you, but when everything started going wrong in my life, I began to blame you. I began to question whether or not you were real. Inside I am hurt and broken, and I need for you to heal it, I need you to heal my heart from all the fake love and betrayal. I know there's someone out there that loves me, and I know you will send them my way to save me from this dark place that I'm in. I know you will because I know it was you that sent my dad back into my life. In Jesus name, Amen!

Just as I got up, my phone chimed, alerting me of a text from Cassidy, letting me know she was staying by her grandmother's. I had to thank God once more for Cassidy because I really 'didn't think I would've gotten this far without her being in my life. Before moving out here, all I had was my parents. All my life it had been just us. I laid in bed, thinking about how good life used to be before drifting off to sleep.

"Ugh!" I jumped up out of my sleep, screaming immediately, balling up in a knot, as Gus continually swung on me with an extension cord. But even through that pain it still had no comparison from the daggers he through at my heart.

"Bitch, you thought it was over!" I started squeezing my eyes tighter, praying it would soon be over. I felt my skin ripping apart with each swing, and I felt the blood drip out of my wounds. I had just prayed and here I was once again, being dealt a badass hand.

I flinched as he turned me over on my stomach because I knew what may come next. After showering, I just laid in the bed naked, and I didn't think Gus would come and fuck with me after my dad showed his face earlier, so I didn't think me not changing the locks would be a problem. Even with everything he had done and put me through, I still thought I would be safe with him. I never in my mind questioned if he would turn around and do the very thing I feared the most. After he beat and pulled his dick out of me, he put his clothes on, and left the same way he came.

I felt dirty, scared, and every inch of my body was aching. I grabbed the bloody towel that laid beside me and wrapped it around my body. At the moment, I didn't think about clothes, I was living in fear, so I took a dash for the front door and ran three blocks until I reached Haynes Projects.

At that moment, I believed when my mama said, 'God will bring you through any storm.' Because here I was beaten and battered, but through all the pain, I still heard Meech's voice without even seeing his face. Maybe this was God's way of answering my prayers when I asked him to send someone to save me. I didn't know Meech, but I knew he was saving me the moment he wrapped his arms around me.

4

Meech

I felt like I was being tested today, because I sure was around more than enough drama to say I hadn't even been out for twenty-four hours.

"Paris!" I screamed as I slapped her face a few times. Looking down at her naked body, made me want to kill whatever nigga violated her. She had so much innocence to her, and I could tell she had gotten herself involved with the wrong nigga.

I grabbed her in my arms and ran toward my grandmother's crib. The Haynes Projects were the most ruthless projects in our hood, so I wasn't about to just leave her lying on the ground.

"Cassidy," I screamed soon as I made it in the house.

"Wha"—" she started to say, but stopped when she noticed how badly beaten Paris was.

"What happened to her, Meech?"

"She was running across the court and just collapsed on the ground. Who you think did this to her"?" Instead of answering me, Cassidy grabbed her phone from her back pocket, and told someone to meet us at the hospital. She ran to the back of the house, retrieving something to put on Paris, and we both ran out the door.

Paris had yet to move her body since she passed out. I laid her head across my lap in the backseat and made a promise to myself to kill whatever nigga had done this to her. The rest of the ride to the hospital, I sat in silence with murder on my mind.

"How long has this been going on?"

We had been sitting in the room for over thirty minutes and hadn't heard anything yet. On top of that, Paris hadn't had any family come to even check on her. Whoever that nigga was Cassidy called was a no call, no show.

"For a while… at first, it was little licks, but she managed to hide them well, and say everything would get better. The day you came home, he was outside our place with another female. She lost a lot behind him, so for that, she doesn't really tell me much about her personal business with Gus"—"

"With who?" I asked, cutting her off.

"His name is Gus; she met him a few years ago, and her dad made her choose between the two of them. She chose to be with Gus, and he had been giving her pure hell since then. She would often say he blamed her for not being able to find work, but she just wanted him to love her the way she loved him."

"Whose shawty pops?" I had a feeling I knew who her dad was. Thinking back to her dad, he appeared in the projects in the middle of her fight. I just didn't put the shit together until now.

"That's him right there"," she said, nodding her head towards the entrance where King and Dino were walking in. He never mentioned he had a daughter. Hell, to be honest, I had never been to his house. I knew of Queen, his wife, but he had never spoken of his daughter. But now,

I see why, niggas would take advantage once they found out she was the daughter of King Malachi.

"I had something to take care of, how is she?" King was dressed in all black and so was Dino, and Cassidy probably was blind to the obvious. But I knew what kind of business he went and handled.

"Family of Paris Lee?"

"Yes, I'm her father!"

"I'm Dr. Blake, and I took care of your daughter when she came in, Mr. Lee. She's a very strong girl. She suffered a lot of internal bleeding, but we were able to stop it and get it under control. She has a few cracked ribs and a fractured eye socket. Ms. Lee, may need counseling in the future, she was raped and from that she has severely scarred tissue and it may be hard for her to have kids in the future."

"When can we see her"?" I found myself asking.

"You can go back there now, she's a very strong girl, and is going to be just fine. She will need as much love and support as she can get from everyone." King shook hands with the doctor and held his head down in pity.

"Go check on, Paris, Cassidy. I'll be in there soon. I need to holla at Meech about something."

We both waited until the halls were clear before speaking to one another.

"I never got a chance to welcome you home!"

"You know I ain't tripping on that."

"Yeah, but I got that bag for you as promised and that seat at the table." I looked up at King for the first time, in five years, and smiled. I was down for five years and not one of those years did he pick up the phone or even came for a visit. I started to think he had abandoned me, but that was apart of our plan.

The five-year bid, I did was for him, he promised me

15

$1.5 million when I came home and the throne over his cartel if I set for him. I would've taken it for nothing because King took care of me and kept me with the newest everything. What people 'didn't know was that King was driving the car that night, and I was on the passenger side when the police got behind us. Instead of stopping, he made a run for it until we were in a dark alley. He promised me everything and got out the car, I got in the driver seat, drove out the alley, and surrendered.

"I know I promised to step down soon as you got out, but I'm not going anywhere until I have Gus's head."

"If he knows what's good for him, he would be running for his life."

"Gus, knew he touched gold when he violated my princess. But I know he's coming for war no matter how much of a lame the bitch is. He don't back down; I know he's coming back."

"What makes you so sure?"

"I violated him like he did me, only I left nobody behind to tell a story."

"Tell them Zoes to' get war-ready!" he said, speaking of my Haitian family.

"We always war-ready, Boss."

"You the boss now son, and I noticed you were really concerned about my daughter."

Paris was fine, but I wasn't checking for her like that. I had Tosha's crazy ass, and I was still dealing with that at the moment, and I didn't want to bring any more drama her way. It was crazy how much I used to love Tosha, it was no woman out here, I put above her. That time behind bars showed me that I was all I got out here. Once I was ready to talk, I would then grace her with my presence.

I decided to walk in the room with King to see Paris before I went to handle a few things. Gus will indeed see me sooner than he thought, but right now, I had more things to focus on. I'll handle him and my friendly pussy ass baby mama when they least expected it.

"I'm sorry, Dad. I should have listened; I know you only wanted what was best for me." Seeing Paris breakdown as soon as King stepped in the room would make any man weak. That's why I didn't blame him when I saw him shedding tears.

"Shhhh, baby girl, I'm just happy to have you back." King was one of the most ruthless, and heartless niggas I knew. But everybody had a weakness and Paris was King's weakness. No wonder he hid her ass for all those years.

"Come on, Cassidy, let's leave them alone."

I'd be sure to check on Paris later, but right now, I had my own problems and things to handle. First thing, was copping me a new crib. My baby moms was in my old one and with that bag King had for me; it was time I copped something much bigger. I most definitely was a boss and it was time I lived like one. I loved my grandmother, but staying with her was a big ass negative.

After everything I had going on was settled, then I would remind these niggas that Big Meech was back. I was out and not here to play with these niggas, I would remind them of what territory is for who, and I didn't give a fuck who I had to kill in the process. They would soon understand that I wasn't that nigga to play with.

5

King Malachi

Baby girl thought I threw her away, but I had been watching her since the day she stepped foot out of our home. Her mother 1 had run herself sick being worried about Paris, and all she did was drink. I hated to throw my only child out there to survive on her own. But I knew dealing with a nigga like Gus would backfire. However, I didn't think it would take three years for her to open her eyes, and I damn sure ain't think it would land her in the hospital.

"Dad, I'm really sorry!"

"No; I'm the one that's sorry. I knew the only reason he was with you was to get to me, but I knew you loved him. This is why I kept you inside to protect you from niggas like Gus. So many days, I would see you unhappy, and I would walk away thinking you would soon come around."

"I was happy at first, but then, I slowly became lonely."

There was a time in life when my daughter was so happy and a free spirit. These days, she talked with her head hanging low. As a man, I felt as if I had failed her, and I was supposed to protect her. Instead, I threw her out there on her own.

"Get some rest, and I'll be back later"." I kissed her on her forehead and exited the room.

Whenever Paris got discharged, she would be coming back home. I was about to hit up Dino to go clean out that place she was leaving in and return her things to her living quarters in our home. My daughter had been through enough, and I'm sure this time around she had learned her lesson. If she hadn't learned, I bet Gus did, and I knew for certain he wouldn't touch anything with King' running through it.

Hopefully, with our daughter being home, I would finally have my Queen in no time. I had called her on the way from the hospital and gave her the good news. I heard the excitement in her voice, so I knew things were about to be back how they were. Queen was a beautiful woman in and out, but she was not the same woman I married when I was a teenager.

I headed to the barbershop where I covered up my money first, then to the warehouse where I kept my dope to make sure everything was looking good. I was in my late 'forties, but I had been running these dusty ass streets since I was fifteen years old. I was getting tired of this game, and I wanted out; it was time for me to relax and enjoy life with my family.

With Meech home, I knew I would soon be able to enjoy all those times I had been rambling about. I had done some fucked up shit since and had seen even worse, but the only thing in life that I regretted was the way I had done my daughter. I've killed a muthafucka in cold blood and sleep peacefully, but watching my daughter suffer brought me to a dark place and broke me down as a man.

But I had something for Gus's ass; his beef was with me, but he took it out on my daughter because his broke ass wanted my reaction.

6

Gus

As a man my soul was hurting before going to Paris's crib. I had every voice in my head saying don't do it. But those lines I had just snorted said something else. I knew fucking with the daughter of King would be dangerous, but at least, I let her live. This nigga killed the only two people that meant something to me. He killed my mother and my girl—she was pregnant and that still didn't stop him.

Even though I had brought all of this on myself by fucking with Paris, he should have just gotten at me. They didn't deserve to die the way they died. I had been with Cola since we were kids and she understood that what I had going on with Paris was for us to live better. I didn't think shit would go the way it did.

I only stayed with Paris as long as I did because I felt bad for her, she was young and naïve. The girl just wanted to be loved and didn't want nothing more than that. I tried to push her away by not showing her any attention, but even then, she stayed. Paris was loyal and someone would be lucky to have her, but Cola had always been my heart and no woman could change that.

I had no remorse or resentment towards Paris. Now that I think about the shit, I had done to her, it wasn't called for. But I wasn't thinking at the time, and I didn't think she would beat Cola's ass the way she did. I had played a dangerous game of life and death. I never really loved Paris, but staying with her was out of guilt because she disobeyed her father to be with me.

Just thinking about what I put Cola through made me break down. After everything, she had stayed by my side and still believed in me; she never once cheated on me because of what I was doing. She was innocent, and someone had to pay for what they had done to her. They took my girl, and I was about to make the streets bleed. King Lee pumped fear in every other nigga, except for me. He would see me again.

***

A Week Later

COLA DIDN'T REALLY HAVE family, so I did her memorial service and my moms together. She held our baby girl in her arm as she laid in the casket, the three of them looked as if they were peacefully sleeping. Shit was so unreal up until today, I was waiting for my mom to scream the food was done. I wanted to think they had taken a nice vacation, but we know that wasn't true.

"They took the most important people in my life. How can I go on?" I said to my childhood friend, Jep. He had flown in the day before to be by my side as I buried my family. Jep was what you considered lucky in the hood, he was indeed a street nigga that did what he could to keep food on the table. But his sick skills in football got him a

22

free ride out. That nigga left and never looked back. The rest of us weren't so fortunate.

"I can't say I know the feeling because I don't; the shit really fucked up. But you already know how this street shit goes. You started this war when you fucked over King and touched his most precious jewel. You violated her, but you better hope and pray they don't find out you were the real reason Meech had to do all that time."

"Fuck King and that hoe Paris. I hit the hoe, I didn't kill her, and King was supposed to do that time, not Meech."

When I planted the drugs in King's car, I expected him to go to jail. I figured if he was in jail Paris would be forced to take over; she knew a little something but not much. I would step up to help her, then take over the throne, but that didn't go as plan when Meech was the one in the car that night and he took the charge.

"Think about your future and come up with a plan. Word on the streets is King put a big bounty on your head and Meech is coming with them Zoes'." I looked at Jep with two heads because there was no way King would come after me. The nigga had knocked out the only family I had, if he was still gunning for me, then this was more personal than I thought.

"I'm not scared of no fucking Meech." "My heart fluttered with fear because there was no doubt in mind that he wasn't coming.

"Well, I have a flight to catch." I dapped my brother down before he jumped out of the car and proceeded to his.

Jep left the hood and was doing damn good for himself. I refused to be the one to bring him down and put him in a fucked-up situation. His whole family was depending on him, and I had put myself in this situation, so I would figure it out alone.

7

Paris

Meech and I had gotten close since my incident, and I hated to feel as if I was dragging him in my mess when I barely even knew anything about him. But every time we saw each other, he would assure me that things were fine. Mentally and emotionally, I was fucked up whenever I thought about the fact that I may never be able to have kids. I no longer felt like a real woman because I would never be able to give a man all of me, only half.

There were days, I would just sit and stare at Meech. He was the perfect man, but, yet, a thug ass nigga. He was about six-foot even, he had dreads that he kept neatly groomed, and his beard was always lined to perfection. He had one dimple in his right cheek and he blessed us with a mouth full of diamonds whenever he smiled. I loved everything about him and hardly knew him, but he hadn't left my side since the day he carried me into the hospital. I know we were just friends and he hadn't crossed any lines with me, but my soul screamed this man's name.

"You cool, P?" Meech asked as he snapped his fingers in front of my face, bringing me from my thoughts.

"Yeah, just in deep thought." I opted not to tell him what I was thinking about. I had been hurt to my worst point lately, and I didn't want to run him off. I had accepted my fault in what went on between Gus and I because I should've been saw the signs. But I refused to place myself in another fucked-up situation.

Speaking of Gus, I wanted to so badly to reach out to him when I heard the news about his mother, but I knew that would be a bad idea. Ms. Gloria treated me like I was her own child whenever I went around there, and to hear that someone had murdered her, and Cola had done something to me. I heard he was going through it hard, and I didn't want to believe it was his karma, but I knew it was no other way around it.

"Why you always avoid me when I ask you certain questions? I understand that you've gone through a lot, but don't let what happened to you be the reason you hold your head down. You are beautiful inside and out, always make eye contact when you are speaking to someone","" he said right before putting his finger under my chin, and lifting my head up.

At that moment, I looked him in his eyes, and they were low from the weed, but I noticed he had a glow to them. I took that as an opportunity to go in for a kiss. I don't know what had come over me, but with Meech it was where I was supposed to be. It all felt so right, but when he pulled away and looked at me like I had lost my mind, I started to regret the decision I had made.

"I'm sorry!"

"I knew y'all was fucking!" Cassidy said, causing me to be more shame than I already was.

"I'm about to get up outta here and handle some business."

Cassidy and I both sat in silence until Meech was

completely out of the house. I knew once he was gone, she would grill me with questions. But there was nothing to talk about. I wanted him, but he saw me as nothing more than a friend.

"Every time I come over here, I can't help but think about how crazy you were for staying in the projects. This bitch is laid the fuck out."

"Yeah, it reminds me how madly in love I was with a nothing ass nigga."

I was happy to be home and even more so happy to be back with my parents. However, it still didn't stop me from thinking about how I spent three years being a fool for a nigga. Maybe it was too soon to fall for Meech, but I just didn't see him doing the same thing Gus had done. I saw him being the one to help my wounds heal.

"Enough of that, you still rolling with me to the block party today"?"

"Yeah, but I ain't driving. I deserve to get fucked up after everything, I had been through."

It was the summertime, so damn near every weekend somebody different was throwing a block party uptown. After what happened the last time, most people would stay far away, but nobody but God pumped fear through my veins

"I know that's right, bitch! Don't get too fucked up, though. Jare got a party at Allure and it's a must we be there."

Cassidy had been having a crush on Jare since we been hanging together. But her ass was always too scared to approach him. If she knew like me, she would go after what the fuck she wanted. Hot girls were taking over this summer.

⊏⊐

PULLING UP TO UPTOWN PARK, we wasted no time parking. I was ready to party, but before I got out, I patted my crossbody to make sure I had my gun on me. Protecting myself and Cassidy was everything to me. After I got caught slipping the last time, I refused to be in that same predicament again.

"This bitch lit!" All the hood niggas and bitches were out today. I even laughed once I saw my dad kneeling down, shooting dice. It didn't matter how much money he had; he was still always in the projects like he had never left. I knew he wanted a son that's why he raised me the way he did. I was humble, but I knew how to cook, flip, score, and sell dope. I just chose to stay in my lane with my makeup and dressing myself up.

I walked over to where he was shooting dice, grabbed his bottle, and went to sit by Cassidy. Checking my surroundings, to make sure nothing was off, I was shocked that I didn't see Meech. But I tried not to hold any emotions on my face. I shrugged my shoulders and continued to laugh and vibe with my best friend.

"Damn, Jare, look better every time I see his ass." I turned to look at Jare, but what crushed me was when I saw Meech leaning on his old school car, gripping a bitch ass. The hurt in my eyes was evident because Cassidy grabbed my hands, pulling them to her chest. I was silly to even think I had a shot with a man like him. He was high powered, and I knew my dad had given him his seat.

Meech was now over my family's cartel, and we could never be nothing more than friends. I released Cassidy's hand and threw me another shot of D'usse back. Luckily, we hadn't done anything, but once again, this was my fault for thinking it could be more than a friendship.

"'I' didn't know he and Jare were friends."

"Best friends since kids."

I nodded my head and continued to vibe to the music; the DJ had shit rolling, and I was in my own zone. The liquor and weed were taking over my body. But no matter how hard I tried to enjoy myself, I couldn't help but to constantly glance over at Meech and the chick he was hugged up with. I couldn't help but to wish I was the one he was hugging on.

Cassidy had gotten the courage and approached Jare. I didn't like the fact that she was over there all buddy-buddy with the chick like she had been knowing her. Since connecting with Jare, the bitch completely forgot I was over here. I knew how bad she wanted that nigga, though, so I ain't trip.

"Alright, baby girl, I'm about to get up out of here, you strapped?"

"Never leave home without her!"

"Niggas will try you because of who your dad is, so never hesitate," he said right before handing me a roll of hundreds. I stood up to hug my dad bye and watched as he walked over to where Meech and Jare were standing.

Meech was with his girl, Cassidy was with her dude, and I was lonely. At this point, it no longer made any sense for me to sit out here. I was seated off by myself and Cassidy had yet to come back over. She had connected with a new love and found a new friend. I was no hater, but I knew it was time I made a move.

I walked over to where they were all standing and told my dad I would catch him home. Meech avoided making eye contact and Cassidy offered to bring me home since I had gone there with her. Without even thinking, I quickly caught an attitude with her. It wasn't meant to be, but more so out of reflex. I walked away and went and sat in the car, waiting for King to finish chopping it up.

The car ride home was so quiet, I decided to pull my

phone out and scroll down social media. Getting on Instagram, the first thing that popped up was a picture Cassidy had posted with her, Jare, Meech and the girl Meech had with him, whose name was Tosha. I wasn't even tripping, but the caption threw me off.

'*You can't sit with us*, 'I thought and laughed out loud. On God, I'll slap that hoe if she throwing shots. Friend or no friend, my feelings were crushed, but instead of being mad or petty, I put my phone on do not disturb and smoked on a blunt with my pops.

"Look, Paris, whatever you do just don't lose yourself again. There was a time in your life when it was hard to wipe your smile away. But as of lately, you walk with a mug and always holding your head down. I noticed the fake shit just like you did tonight, but don't let that hold you back. The daughter of King Malachi will shit on whatever nigga or bitch that crosses her. Let these past few months be a fucking lesson, never shad another tear again."

My dad was right, the last few months had taught me a very valuable lesson about trusting people. I had laid everything on the table and had still been hurt by those I trusted. Whatever happens from this day on out is very personal. There was no beef, no hate, or no war. Just simply looking out for myself.

I walked into the mansion and went to my wing of the house. After showering, I laid in my bed and was in deep thought. I lost myself in Gus. But refused to lose myself in another man. Meech and I had to never see each other again and if we did, I would stay out of his way. I wish I would have never kissed him, then maybe I wouldn't be so driven about him being with another woman. I never fucked him, so I didn't even understand why I was tripping so hard.

It was time to get back to loving me. Focusing on me,

and more importantly getting back to building my very own Paris Narcole brand. The next man I catch feelings for won't be able to walk all over me as easily. Right now, I was feeling like fuck everybody, except for King and Queen Lee.

━━━

A WHOLE MONTH had passed since I last saw or talked to both Meech and Cassidy. The next morning, after the block party, I had a bunch of missed calls and text messages from them both. Cassidy apologized and deleted the picture. She really had nothing to feel guilty about, all I did was like the picture, but I hadn't even spoken on it.

Meech, on the other hand, was drunk and pouring his feelings out. Talking about he had only brought her out there, thinking it would change how he felt about me. He couldn't date the daughter of his boss, but that excuse was bullshit. It was bullshit because he was the boss now. I was good on the fake shit from the both of them.

He and Jare spent a lot of time at the crib. Most days, I would avoid going on the other side of the house, then other days, I would walk straight past him as if he was invisible. Lately, I had been so deep into opening my boutique that their betrayal no longer bothered me.

"Today's the big day, huh?" my mother said as she walked into my living quarters. I was letting Ameerah do my hair while MakeupbyDaria was beating my face. Today, I was having my grand opening at the mini-mall I had purchased.

"Yes, I'm so excited!"

"I'm proud of you, Princess."

"I know, but please, don't make me cry while I'm

getting my make up done or later. I know how you get, and I'm not trying to mess my face up before the after-party."

"Can't wait until the after-party."

"AHT, AHT! You are not coming, it bad enough ya husband is going to be there."

8

Meech

I 'WAS A BRICKLAYER, YOU WANTED A PILL SELLER

Bitch, you was my girl, I give you the world
Seem like you rather struggle
Say you wanted to be in love, but you wasn't ready for it
You left a nigga with metric tons to be with a petty hustle—'

I was on my way to Paris's grand opening, listening to Kevin Gates. It was crazy how this nigga had a song that described everybody's life in some way or another. The "World Luv" had put me in my feelings every time I listened to it. Because no matter how bad I wanted Paris, I just wasn't ready for her.

Sexually, I had never touched her, but mentally and emotionally, she was already my wife and she didn't even know it. A whole month without any contact had gotten my mind right. The night she walked away from the block party was the last time, I had heard her voice. Whenever I was over at her crib, she would be in and out as if I wasn't in the room. I had hurt her trying to escape the lust I had for her.

"I should've never posted that picture"," Cassidy said

as I parked my car on the curb and gave the valet driver my keys. I don't know what the fuck her motive was when she posted that picture and added that caption, but she was indeed tripping.

The line to get in was wrapped around the building. Cassidy and I walked the red carpet and stopped for a picture before entering the party. To my surprise, we were both placed on the VIP list.

"Yeah, that picture is what cost you your friendship. You never even liked Tosha, so I was confused as to why were you even acting buddy-buddy out there. You left your girl on the side as if she wasn't even with you"," I said in between smiles; she brought her situation with Paris on herself. But wanted someone to feel sorry for her.

"Ok, we are done," the picture man said, and we walked off to head into the party. I was in no mood to further talk about Cassidy and her feelings, because I didn't really blame P for not fucking with her.

I had to admit, I was proud of Paris and how far she's come in a month. Watching her smile and interact with people in the room was breathtaking. The girl, I met a month ago was hurt and full of pain, you couldn't pay her to smile or hold her head up. When I got to know who she really was, I knew then money didn't buy happiness, she had more than enough and left it all behind for love.

"I'm so proud of her"." Cassidy had been a bit depressed since the picture move, she pulled. She had finally gotten Jare to notice her, but even he was looking at her sideways. The move she pulled would make any nigga reconsider, if you can't be loyal to your only friend, then how could you be trusted.

"Go over there and congratulate her then!"

Walking over to her, I noticed how her smile semi faded, but then came back as she reached out and hugged

Cassidy. Maybe, she missed her friend as well or maybe she just didn't want to cause a scene at her new business. Whatever it was, if I was Paris, I'd keep Cassidy close and watch her. She was my cousin, but even when we were kids, she made some snake moves.

"Hey, everyone, I 'was to thank you all for coming out to the opening of Paris World. I couldn't have done any of this without God and my parents. I remember being lost, not knowing what I wanted out of life, or even if I wanted to live any longer. A friend of mine lifted my chin up and told me some words that I would never forget. For that, I thank him as well. Now shop, eat, and meet me at Allure for my after-party." I looked at her with the biggest smile on my face before throwing my shot back.

"Beautiful speech!"

I stood over Paris's short but perfect frame, congratulating her on her accomplishments. But from the look she gave me, I knew I had hurt her. None of it was intentional, though, and I hope she would soon forgive me.

"I just wanted to come over and tell you how proud I was of you before I head out."

"Thanks, Meech!"

Damn, she was being cold towards me!

Without saying another word, I left out the party and headed home with thoughts of Paris invading my mind. She was so pure and different, I wanted nothing more than to take her away from her hurt and protect her. But I guess, I had caused her to hurt more than she always was.

Tosha had been blowing my phone up, trying to get me to come to her crib. There was nothing between us anymore, though. I stopped fucking with her after the block party that night. But using her as a game had her thinking, we would get back together. The only thing left there was a child and the older Jordan got, the more I noticed she looked nothing like me.

—

LOOKING AT MY CLOCK, I noticed it was almost one in the morning. Jare and Cassidy had both been blowing me up, so I decided to get up and throw something on. No matter how distant P was being with me, I was still going to support her with whatever she had going on. But after the way she played me earlier, I just wanted to stay home.

I wasn't in the mood for dressing up, so I threw on a black Lacoste shirt, some black straight fitting jeans, and a pair of black Gucci shoes. I pulled my dreads in a high bun, and I decided not to put that much jewelry on. I wasn't your typically Kingpin, and you wouldn't know I had money galore just by looking at me. The diamond-encrusted watch and chain were enough. A dab of Versace cologne, and I was out the door.

9

Paris

I was at the club twerking to Meg thee Stallion. My VIP section was full of family, friends, strippers, and some of my dad's workers. I was having a blast and lately, I had been feeling more and more like a boss. Looking around me, I had to thank God for everything and answering my prayers, to bring my father back into my life.

Day so hard so much stress life won't let up boy, just rest lay down, and let me cover you with all these kisses.

The D'usse had taken a toll on me because one minute I was being a hot girl, then the next I was looking Meech in his eyes as he walked into the section, singing Tammy Rivea. I had missed our talks and was mad at myself for being so cold with him earlier. But I honestly didn't know what to say, the shit had hurt me deep. If I forgave Cassidy, I'm sure, I could forgive him as well.

"Let's go upstairs to the office and talk." My father owned majority of the shit in Baton Rouge and Allure just happened to be one.

"I'm sorry, bruh!" Meech spoke soon as I closed the door behind me.

I was drunk and horny, so I didn't answer. I walked over to him and began to kiss him. Surprisingly, he accepted my tongue, he tasted so good; it was a mix of gum and weed. His hands felt good against my body and he felt all over my body.

I slid my dress down my body, and kicked my heels off. I laid on the sofa that sat in the corner and began to move my fingers in and out of my opening. Bringing my fingers up to my mouth and tasting my own sweet nectar, I watched as Meech dropped his pants and grabbed the monster he walked around with daily. He positioned himself between my legs and slowly slid in me until I felt him whole.

"Damn, P!" Him sliding in and out of me was the best feeling ever. Nothing could be heard in the room, except for moans and the sound of my wetness splashing against his stomach. Meech's dick was at least ten inches and my pussy was taking all of that big muthafucka.

"Fuck, I'm about to nut, bae." I was at my peak when he pulled out of me and began to eat me. I damn near lost my mind trying to get away from him, but he grabbed my waist and nibbled on my clitoris until I was squirting everywhere. He slid right back in until he got his nut.

"Damn, Paris, you been holding back, huh?" I didn't respond because I knew I had done a damn good job. I went into the restroom and washed myself up. Putting our clothes back on, we were back in the section, partying with everyone else.

"You coming home with me tonight," Meech screamed over the music.

"Yep!"

"You know you mine, right?" Meech leaned down and kissed me as if we were the only ones in the room.

"Damn, so you being here with another bitch is more important than being home with me and your daughter"?" Meech and I were walking out the club, hand in hand, when Tosha and her gang decided to roll up on us. I knew some bullshit would come tonight. I was shocked as fuck to hear that Meech had a child, though.

"Chill, you embarrassing yourself and drawing too much attention. You know I don't move like that."

"Boy, fuck how you move."

I could see the anger radiating off Meech, so I grabbed his hand and tried pulling him away from the drama. Tosha was indeed doing too much in front of all these people. But I was doing the same thing a few months ago. This time she's in the same position, I stood in when I saw Cola and Gus together.

"Jarcole, if you leave with her that would be the worse mistake of your life."

"Nah, the worse mistake of my life was putting my trust in a hoe like you. I will make an appointment to get that DNA test handled, then we would go from there"," he said as he started to walk away.

"Are you serious right now, blood? That bitch got your head that far gone?" Tosha had one more time to call be a hoe, or bitch, before I went upside her head.

"Please, Meech, don't do this to me. Don't do this to us."

At this point, she was basically on her knees, begging, and her friends were all standing around her with pity looks on their faces. I felt bad for her because I know how it felt to want somebody that 'didn't want you. I stood there staring at her while Meech tried to ply her hands from around his legs.

39

"Handle this!" King demanded Meech right before grabbing my hand and pulling me towards the car. Since the Gus situation my father didn't take playing with me lightly, and he didn't care who you were. He was overprotective, and I honestly didn't blame him.

I looked back a Cassidy before getting in the car, and we both held a look of sympathy in our eyes. It's crazy how life worked every time I open up my mind to Meech something stands in the way. I had just given this man all of me and walked out of the club to baby mama drama.

This time around, I wasn't mad or hurt because I know what it was like to be in love. I knew what it was like when you wanted something so bad, but you could never have it. I wouldn't fight this time around, I would just sit back and let the universe take over.

"You hungry?" my dad asked, and I nodded my head. We went to Waffle House and damn near ordered the whole menu while talking about everything under the sun. I was happy to have my dad back in my life, because it was the talks, I missed the most. Most girls wouldn't be comfortable with smoking with their parents. Well, mine would light the blunt up first and pass it my way.

THE NEXT MORNING, I woke up with a massive headache. Right when I was about to get up, to handle my hygiene, my phone started going off like crazy with text messages. I can't believe I had felt bad for Tosha, and she got on social media and degraded my character as a woman. I was beyond pissed off because it was bitches up there that knew nothing about the situation, but had the nerve to vouch with that bullshit.

"Stupid bitch!" I screamed out loud while jumping

from the bed to put some black tights on. If I didn't kill this bitch, I would kill this hoe soon.

Last night, I walked away from the club and left Meech there to handle Tosha. But for the hoe to get on social media, and disrespect me was a big ass negative and unacceptable. This bitch had my picture all over her page, and bitches were hating, and niggas were trying to get put on. But she had just signed up for an ass whopping.

"Bitch, come get me!" I screamed into the phone soon as Cassidy answered.

"Already outside."

I threw some tights and tennis on, then went to handle my hygiene before running down the stairs. When I got to the door, my mother was standing in the foyer, dressed like she had murder on her mind with a bat in her hand. I knew then shit was about to be crazy.

"Somebody sent me the screenshots, and I been waiting for your ass to come down here."

We both jumped in the car with Cassidy and made our way to the Haynes Projects. hoes like Tosha needed to die because they didn't know how to stay off social media. I didn't know what went down with her and Meech because I left. But instead of her going after him, she came after me. People need to stop letting my pretty face and height fool them.

Meech had been blowing my phone up all morning, but I didn't want to talk. Control your bitch, then we would have something to talk about. I'll really murk that girl, and for her to be playing with me on social media, after, I felt bad for her really had me pissed the fuck off.

Just as we whipped down by the basketball court, Meech and Tosha were standing outside fussing. The car was barely in park before I jumped out and ran to where the two of them were standing. Queen jumped out and followed behind me. She knew just like I did that Tosha wasn't about to post anything about anybody else on social media.

"The fuck you come over here for, bitch? I guess you about to beg me to take that shit off social media like your pussy ass boyfriend, huh?"

"Cass, pull ya phone out and go live because this bitch loves a show, so give her one."

Soon as those words left my mouth, I cocked back and drew down on Tosha's face, instantly drawing blood. I wasn't the one to talk, and with one lick, she was on the ground. I stood over her and continued to throw punches to her face. I wanted to kill the bitch, but I knew that wasn't the route to take.

"Break the bitch neck, P!" I heard my mama screaming as I stood over Tosha, stumping her out. I drew my foot back one last time, but Meech picked me up and carried me away. Tosha was no match for me, and I'm sure she would have nothing else to say about little ole me again.

"I thought you were different, Paris!"

"Different how?"

"You out here in the middle of the projects, fighting like some hood rat. Tosha has nothing to lose while you got everything to lose."

I looked at Meech and walked off, he was in my face, calling me out for beating a bitch's ass that had humiliated me on social media. I was tired of letting people slide because I had an image to protect. Fuck that! If I feel any type of way, somebody was going to feel me, and I meant that shit.

10

Meech

I was in the middle of the basketball court, fussing with Tosha about posting a picture of Paris on facebook. Last night, I had made love to Paris, and I would be a damn fool if I was to ever let that good ass pussy go anywhere. I had everything under control, but I didn't expect to see Paris jump out of the car and began to fight Tosha.

Never in a million years did I want to see my girl out here fighting. Then, she had the nerve to get mad at me, but what took the cake was when I saw Queen standing there, coaching her. Call me what you want, but I immediately grabbed my phone and placed a call to King. I left Tosha right where she was because she deserved everything she had gotten.

"What's good, young blood?" he said into the receiver.

"I can't call it. but you talked to Queen or Paris today!"

"Yeah, Queen called me from the jail. I'm about to go post bail on them now. Obviously the bitch called the police and they went picked them up from the house. I don't like the pigs snooping around where I lay my head, they start to ask questions. Meet me at the police station and call Jare to get his girl. I know that's your cousin, but something about her rubs me wrong

I ain't answer him back because I felt the same way he did. I placed that call to Jare and made my way to the prison to get my baby. She had fucked up earlier, but I was not about to let her sit in that bitch another minute, or I would be a damn fool if I allowed her to sit another hour.

When the three of them walked from the back, I could've punched Paris ass down for smiling so hard. Jare came to post Cassidy's bail and left before she was processed out. He and her were completely opposite, he was so low key with everything he did. He was always making money and going home. They were too damn old to be in the middle of the projects fighting like they didn't have shit to lose.

"Come on!" I grabbed Paris's hand and pulled her out of the jailhouse. I didn't fuck with pigs and she knew that. So, that alone had me pissed that I had to come up here and get her ass. I know she was fucked up, but she really needed to change her ways because she was too beautiful.

Soon as I pulled off from the prison, I turned the music all the way up, and lit a blunt, purposely not passing it to her. I ignored the way she was looking out the window, pouting. Paris was spoiled out the gate, and she expected everybody to bow down to her and cater to her when she was wrong. I understand Tosha was fucked up for putting her picture on Facebook. But how you leave a damn mansion to go fight a bitch in the projects.

"I'm going to shower," she said soon as we got in the house. While she showered, I made it a point to call Jare and Dino to let them know they needed to handle every-thing today. Me and my girl needed to spend some much-needed time together since she wanted attention so bad.

I took off my clothes and got in the bed, preparing to find us a movie to watch on Netflix.

"You are a little too comfortable!" she said with an attitude as she came out the bathroom with a towel wrapped around her body.

Hands down, Paris was the baddest and most beautiful woman, I had ever laid my eyes on. Her skin was smooth and the beads of water that rolled down glowed upon her. She had a towel wrapped around her body and her hair hung down the sides of her face. I sat up on the side of the bed, and grabbed her hands, pulling her towards me.

"I love you, yeah, and I know it may be hard to believe since we haven't known one another that long. But being with you is where I belong."

"Well, why is it so hard to be with just me?"

"You serious right now? You just beat the fuck out of Tosha, and I left her on the ground to come and be with you. If I wanted other women, then I would be with other women, instead of being here with you."

This time, I planted my lips on hers, not giving her a chance to speak or say anything else to ruin the moment. She grabbed my dreads, causing her towel to drop to the floor. I pulled back and took in her beauty before laying her back on the bed and spreading her legs apart. Her yoni was freshly waxed, and she smelled like cocoa butter.

I pushed her legs apart and parted her clit, moving my tongue in a circular motion before sucking on her. Her legs started shaking as she arched her back and began to cum in my mouth over and over again.

"What are you doing to me?"

"Relax, bae, let me take care of you."

I leaned against her body and inserted my tip into her while covering her mouth with mine before digging deep into her guts. Paris pussy was so tight and fresh it would make any man lose his mind. Gus was crazy because after getting it, I think I was stuck. She let out soft moans as she enjoyed every wave, I took her on.

This wasn't ordinary sex, our souls connected with each movement. I made love to her because I had hurt her before even making things official with her. I never knew how connected I was to her until we went a whole month without talking.

"I'm sorry for earlier"," she moaned in between strokes.

"I love you, Meech, shit, it feels so good."

"I love you too, bae"," I spoke right before I nutted in her.

I loved Paris, but I knew, I still had Tosha to deal with. She had been sending threats to my phone since I left her on the ground earlier. I guess what Paris had done to her wasn't enough, but she just didn't know, I would bury the bitch before I let her ruin my happiness. The rest of the night, we watched movies and made love. One day, in the future, Paris would be my wife, but for now, I would just enjoy her being by my side.

11

Cassidy

"She stays over there"," I said to Paris.

My man hadn't been home since he bailed me out of jail, a week ago. The crazy thing is I wasn't even fighting, but since I was the driver and recorded the fight, I got locked up too. He didn't even wait for me to come from the back, I had to catch an Uber home.

I still had my apartment in the projects but from time to time I would stay by Jare's house. About two days ago, I decided to pop up at his house because I was tired of him ignoring me, but I was shocked as fuck when the locks were changed on me. I knew he was mad, but damn, did he really have to go that damn far.

"How do you know he's over here?"

"The girl, Jaymi, posted a picture of him in her bed asleep, and his truck is parked right there in the front yard." I didn't even know I was friends with a bitch name Jaymi on Facebook, but I guess she would only stalk my profile to keep up with me and my man. Typical hood bitch, so I couldn't even trip.

"You got Bella?"

"Never leave home without her."

We got out the car and went around the back of the house. I used to pick the lock to get in my grandmother's house when she locked the door on us, so I knew exactly what I was doing. I had picked the lock at the back door and gained entry into the home. Paris had her gun raised while I walked behind her, looking from room to room.

"Hand me your gun!" She did as I said, without asking any questions. I reached for the door where I heard moans and bust in there with my gun raised. I watched the same bitch that posted my man, riding his dick as he laid there like a king.

"Damn, this what we doing now? We have a little disagreement and you in another bitch bed."

"Come on, Cass, your tripping; let's talk about his at home." Jare's voice disgusted me when he began to speak.

"The same home you put me out of?" He couldn't be talking about that home.

"He changed the locks because I told him to, he's miserable being with you. Playtime is over and its time for him to come back home to me, love." Jaymi got out the bed, placed a robe on, and started walking towards me.

At this point, Paris had come in the room, and stood beside me. The gun was still raised, and my finger was on the trigger. Somebody in here had to die for fucking with my feelings.

"I can't believe, I'm around here carrying your baby and you laid up with another bitch."

"Girl, get a grip on life out here lying about being pregnant, and if you are a baby cant keep no damn man. Never could, and never will."

"Chill, Jaymi!" Jare screamed while getting dressed.

"Fuck her and that baby, that hoe lying. The bitch is looney, and I can prove it"," she said as she walked away to grab her phone. I reached in my back pocket and through the test at Jare before shooting Jaymi in her head, and watching it explode like a watermelon.

"'Bout time you popped hat hoe, she talks too damn much." Paris said with a laugh.

"Jare as bad as I want to send you with her, I don't want to explain to my child why their father is no longer with us. Clean this bullshit up and watch them dog ass hoes you lay with." I just stood there looking at him, I had tears rolling down my face and my heart was full of hurt.

"Come on, Cassidy, let Jare take care of this." I looked up at Paris, and I could tell she felt sorry for me. But as quickly as I went in, I left out. Soon as I slid down in the seat of the car, I released all the tears I had in me.

After carefully thinking over what happened between Jare and I, I decided getting an abortion might be what's best. I was nervous as hell, walking into the clinic. People were outside with Bible scriptures and the whole time I walked in; I held my head down. Paris had her own problems, so I was on my own today, I had no one else to call on.

I know I haven't been a good friend lately, but I was trying to correct my wrongdoings. I was trying to gain her trust back. She was my only friend and had been here in my corner since going through everything. She had her own wing in her parents' house and suggested I move in with them.

When I walked into the clinic, I went straight to check in, and took a seat. Coming here was embarrassing, and Lord knows, I wanted my baby. But I didn't want he or she being in a fucked-up situation. I didn't know if I was doing this to hurt Jare, or because I was hurt about what I had seen earlier.

"You sure this what you want to do, because you don't

seem so sure." I held my head down the whole time I sat there, waiting for my name to be called. Jare standing over me must have been my sign from God. I was trying to abort my baby for all the wrong reasons.

"I honestly don't know, I thought me doing this would be what's best for the both of us."

"Since when did you start thinking for me? I never said, I didn't want my baby. You made that decision on your own."

"Yeah, But"—"

"But nothing! You caught me down bad, and for that, I'm sorry. I rather you beat my ass, then kill my seed","" he said, cutting me off.

Lately, my emotions had been over the place, so I began to cry when Jare was talking to me. I didn't think me coming here would hurt him as much as it was. Being in the position I was in; I was confused as fuck and didn't know what to think. However, I knew that I didn't want to be a single mother, living out the projects all my life.

"Cassidy Smith!" an older nurse came from the back and called my name. I sat in my seat and began to look from her to Jare. Before I could say anything, he stood to his feet and walked over to the nurse, giving her a couple hundreds, and thanking her.

Truthfully, I no longer wanted Jare because I knew I could no longer trust him. But I would pray that he could be a great father because loving one woman was not the route for him. As we got ready to exit, Gus and Tosha walked in, and I stood behind Jare, looking at them with a confused look.

"Tell Paris consider it an even swap."

"Bitch, that's not even the case, that nigga broke, but I will tell Meech and King, I ran into the two of you." I refused to speak after Jare finished reassuring them Meech would find them, and we walked away.

I couldn't believe they both had stooped so low to hurt Paris and Meech. This life was a crazy one, and I hated that I was about to bring my baby in it. I didn't want my child growing up being apart of a cartel family, but who was I to stop the way of life?

Once we reached our cars, I got in mine and Jare got in his without saying another word. Just as we came, we left. I was cool with us not speaking because it was nothing left between us, and the bed he made, he had to lay in it.

12

Jare

Everybody was starting to piss me the fuck off, and I know I had no reason to be mad. I was more drove than anything, though. Cassidy wasn't fucking with me at all, and my side bitch was dead because my main bitch had killed her. Then the bitch turned around and tried to kill my seed.

Cassidy was tripping, and I couldn't just say fuck Jaymi because she was a runner for us. She knew the shipments like the back of her hand, and cutting her off would be like committing suicide. I knew that rat bitch would go to the people, so I decided to just give her what she wanted to keep her levelheaded. It was nothing more than that, she ain't know nothing about me changing the locks until Cassidy mentioned it.

The morning of her appointment, I went over to talk to her, but as I was turning in, she was leaving out. Imagine how hurt I was when I followed her car from Paris's crib to the clinic. To top things off with her no brain having ass, Tosha and Gus were together. To say he wanted me to get a message back to Meech, they sure fled the scene quick.

These past few days had been so stressful, I ended up giving Jaymi's mama some money to pay for her funeral. I felt bad and responsible even though Jaymi wouldn't stop running her mouth. Had I told the truth; we wouldn't be here right now. I had been stressing about Cassidy not talking to a nigga, especially after finding out she was pregnant.

"I need you to go meet Roscoe with the drop, and pick up some money from Tiny's big ass."

"Bet!"

My mind was everywhere, except on the drug game right now. I had fucked up the best thing that had happened to me. She refused to even look my way when I'm around. Hopefully, one day, should be able to forgive me, but then again, she was tripping too hard.

Later that night, I was chilling by the boat dock, waiting on Roscoe to arrive. Meech figured transporting drugs by boat was better than by car or plane. To me, it was all about who you had doing it, the police would only fuck with the guilty.

"What's good, Jare? King didn't say you would be the one meeting us today"," Roscoe's big country ass said.

"Yeah, well, he and Meech had other obligations." I noticed how Roscoe's mood instantly changed. I regretted coming by myself, but King had been doing business with Roscoe for so long, I didn't think I had anything to worry about.

"So, what you got for me today?"

"Nothing, just 'the same as always; ten kilos of that white gal."

"Ten, huh?"

"Look, you got my money? I'm not in the mood to play with you."

Roscoe began to laugh as his crew followed behind

him, pulling out their guns. "This how we gon' handle this. You gon' give me those bags behind you, and walk away without the money."

"Oh, so, you want a war with King?"

I had to ask because it was no way he would just take these kilos and freely walk the streets without having a death wish. It wasn't good to fully trust people because greed and jealously were some big ass demons. Roscoe carried the monkey on his back and thought the shit was funny.

"You gon' have to take me out, big brother, because there's no way I'm just going to let you leave with the bags."

"I tried to be nice, Jare, I was going to let you live."

"Then that would be stupid on your part," I said before taking a seat on the couch that sat behind me. I pulled the already rolled blunt from behind my ear and crossed my leg over the other. Lately, life had been crazy, and I've had a few weary nights. Death would have to be both of our only way out, because I for damn sure wasn't about to let them just walk away with that much money.

My body erupted like a volcano when the bullets started piercing my body. I looked at Roscoe as he smiled, and I began to smile back. Roscoe had to know I was no sucker ass nigga and Kevin Gates always said, 'you die by the law of which you live.' All the bodies I've caught, and drugs I've sold, I been prepared for the consequences that come with the game.

13

Paris

"Dang, bae, you still mad at me." Meech had been tripping since he found out what Cassidy did. He had punished me from getting Pablo and everything. Pablo was the name; I had given the third leg that sat between his legs. That thing was enough to make any bitch go crazy, and his tongue just sent me overboard.

"Shit was stupid as fuck Paris, then what made it worse was when I was calling your sneaky ass, you refused to answer the phone. You going behind my back and doing shit like that can potentially fuck you up."

I decided to just straddle him, because I had been hearing this same speech since Jare told him Cassidy's nutty ass killed that girl. But I didn't.' My girl thought it was cool just to put you through bullshit and you not react. It didn't' work like that, though, you have to set an example sometimes, and show both males and females not to fuck with you.

I pulled my shirt over my head and watched as Meech took my nipples one by one into his mouth and began to nibble on them. He knew grinding his teeth on my nipples would send me overboard. I quickly pulled my panties to the side and directed his shaft inside of me, not being able to have sex was torturing for me. I had never liked sex as much, so this was all new to me, but I was enjoying it.

Meech's phone kept ringing and it was throwing my concentration off. After the fifth ring, I allowed him to just answer the phone. That was something I had to deal with, with a nigga of his status, but the good thing about it was that most times his workers would do his dirty work, and he'd only go out to get his money. However, that still 'didn't mean anything because there are times when his workers called him all day about petty shit. I see why my mom used to be so upset with my dad.

I'm guessing the phone call was really important because he went on the balcony to answer it. I tried not to be that girl that was insecure, but let's be real, Meech has played me for the fool since the very first time I met him. The time that made the shit even more difficult was the fact that it was with the same bitch. So, he needed to explain to me why I should stick around when he can't keep his dick to himself.

"That call must have been important," I' said as he came back into the room and started to get dressed. The whole time he was putting on clothes, I was pouting and rolling my eyes. I was really starting to become pissed off at his actions.

"Come on, Paris, it's not what you're thinking. That was King on the phone and its something that I need to go handle"," he said before kissing me on the forehead

I knew what I got myself into when I started dealing with him, and I also knew how to deal with it. Him being in the streets working was not my problem because I'm always gone to the shop. My problem is catching him with Tosha after I had just knocked that hoe in her head. I noticed she had been texting and calling him, but all her calls were going unanswered.

A few weeks ago, Meech found out Jordan wasn't his and even though his mouth said one thing, his eyes spoke a different language.

⊏▬▬⊐

I HADN'T EVEN NOTICED, I went to sleep, until my phone started ringing. I looked at my phone and noticed it was my father calling. I prayed like hell nothing was going on.

"What's up, Dad?"

"Your mother there?" I told him to hold on as I went to look on their side of the house. She was nowhere to be found, and I noticed the keys to the second set of cars were missing, which meant she was gone.

"No, she's gone! Is everything ok"?"

"Go get Cassidy, and bring her to the hospital, then go right back home. I'll explain everything later," he said right before hanging up.

I was eager to know what was going on, but I did just as he said and went to pick up Cassidy. On the way over, Meech wasn't answering, so I knew it was something bad. I just hoped and prayed whatever it was that it would come to pass. Shit was getting crazier and crazier by the day.

"Did they say what was going on?"

"No, I was only told to bring you to the hospital and go back home. Something crazy is going on."

I pulled up to the hospital and noticed Meech standing outside on his phone, I didn't even feel like fussing. He saw

I called that phone, but he was out here chatting on it, ignoring me. I let Cassidy out the car and made my way home to see what was going on with my father. If it wasn't one thing with this family, it was another.

14

Meech

"Come on, King, you know Jare wouldn't steal from us, or no one for that matter."

I was going to always stand on all ten and defend Jare, but man, I had sent him to make a drop over ten hours ago, and hadn't heard anything back from him. He wasn't answering the phone. Roscoe wasn't answering the phone, and I was starting to get a badass feeling.

"Then where the fuck is he?"

"I sent Dino to the yacht, so maybe he'll find something."

Just as those words left my mouth, Dino came walking through the warehouse door with blood all over his shirt.

"He still got a pulse, but everything is gone, and they lit him up."

If I had ever questioned God today was not one of those days. I knew for a fact that he was real. No one knew how long he was on the boat like that, but one thing was that Roscoe's ugly ass knew something.

"We gotta get him to a hospital, ASAP."

These days luck wasn't on my side, even though Paris

and I had sex. I still wasn't fucking with her for killing Jare's side bitch, and leaving us behind to clean up their mess. Shit like that was detrimental to the business. Following behind Cassidy's nutty ass was about to have her single.

I jumped in the backseat where Jare was laid out and placed his head in my lap. Since getting in the car King had yet to speak, but from the smug look he had, I knew he was pissed. He was on the phone, texting back and forth about something. A war was brewing and muthafuckas didn't even know what was coming for them.

King had been doing business with Roscoe for as long as I could remember. I didn't want to point fingers, but this had his name written all over it. After all the business deals we cut with that fat bitch, he decided to violate the team and steal.

I ran in the hospital just as Dino pulled up by the emergency room entrance. Running in the hospital full speed, with both me and Dino, we were holding on to Jare. Nurses and doctors rushed to our side, checking Jare's pulse, and taking him to the back. It was crazy how my brother was still holding on.

"You know what this means, right?" I nodded my head and rubbed my hands together. We took a two-million-dollar loss and somebody was about to pay.

"I'll stay until we get word on Jare. Tiny got Roscoe's righthand at the warehouse."

"Him being there is cool, but will he talk? If not, tell Tiny to kill him now. I've wasted enough time, and I'm not trying to waste a minute more."

As long as King took care of me, I had never spoken cruel to him, but I was serious when I said, I was fed the fuck up. I didn't have time to torture a nigga that wasn't going to talk.

"I understand that you are frustrated, but you will fix your tone whenever you talk to me. Jare was special to me as well, but luckily, he had a bulletproof vest on. I guess that lil' nigga wasn't so dumb after all. I will call Paris to bring Cassidy down here, and we will go handle this shit."

I see now where Paris got her fucking ways from. Since knowing King, no nigga alive would make the mistake of playing with his money. They may have gotten out the way with him, but they knew not to touch that money. So, I know to have a close friend do this to him was fucking with him bad.

Jare and I were all we had; we were two young niggas forced to make ends meet. The only difference between the two of us was that Jare's mama died and he never knew his pops. We looked out for each other, and together we couldn't be fucked with.

Too many people were trying to mess with the camp at one time. I still had yet to get at Tosha and Gus, and hearing they were together had me wanting to bust their heads even more. Paris was blowing up my phone and was really starting to piss me off with her insecurities. My nigga almost died and muthafuckas wanted our heads. I just wanna lay up with my girl and run my day down to her, but shit wasn't like that at all.

15

Queen

I was beyond pissed, and I knew if I kept playing this game for too long shit would eventually go left. King spent long hours and plenty of days at the warehouse when he didn't even have to. Him being out, when he held a status that allowed him to stay home, led me to believe he was doing more than just overseeing shipments and money.

"I told you if you didn't leave him that I would do something crazy. I hated that things went the way they did, but he was standing in the way."

"So, basically you wanted King to find out it was you. Roscoe, you didn't think this whole thing through."

"I thought it through, I just didn't expect Jare to be the one to make the drop."

This time around, I had fucked up bad, and was praying like hell that King didn't find out about my affair with Roscoe. I had been sneaking around with him for years and had never gotten caught. Not like he would even find out, being that he was never home, but if he did, I knew he would be crushed.

"I did this for us, Queen, I just wanted us to be together." His words hit me hard and cut me like a sharp knife. At that moment, I felt that I had to protect him from whatever was coming his way. I couldn't just let King kill him. As much as I hated to admit it, I loved Roscoe.

"Look, I'll do as much as I can to protect you, but you need to get away from here quick. You fucked up by touching Jare, and no one knows, but he is the heir to King's cartel."

For years, I had held King's secret by not even telling Paris that Jare was her brother. His mama, Bonnie, and King had a lil' thing going back in the days and she ended up pregnant. King played his part or tried, but Bonnie wanted all of him and not just a piece. She took Jare and left. But it wasn't until she died that Jare came back and King saw him on the corner, hustling and started to take care of him. He made me promise not to say anything, and I did just that.

"Damn, I fucked up, come with me!"

"I can't! King will kill the both of us, and I have to stay and try to calm him down. I know my husband and right now, he is on a rampage."

"Don't call him that while you with me."

Lord, I don't know what made me put this good ass pussy on this man, but he was going crazy. I was so scared of King finding out about my disloyalty, but I never thought things would come to this. I made a vow to my husband, despite whatever he may have done to me as a woman, I was never supposed to break my vows.

I left the hotel Roscoe and I had been meeting up for the past few years, and went home to play nice. A few years ago, you couldn't pay me to be disloyal. Now here I was going against the grain. But if it was to ever hit the surface, I just prayed my daughter would remain the same. She loved the ground her father walked on, though, so I knew once King found out things would be different.

Pulling up home, I sat in the car for a minute, and just looked at my beautiful home. The front room light was on, but things seemed a bit different, it didn't look like home anymore and a sudden feeling of nervousness settled at the bottom of my stomach.

I got out the car, and headed for the door and forced a smile on my face. I was sixteen years old when I met King and even then, he had money. That man took me from the life I hated in Haynes Projects, to the one I had never dreamed of. In return, I betrayed him, but in my defense, he betrayed me first.

Seeing King sitting at the head of our beautiful glass table with blood all over his shirt and bloodshot eyes did something to me. I knew then he was crying over Jare, or he knew something about what happened tonight. His gun sat in the middle of the table while Paris was seated with her back, facing the entrance of the house.

"What's going on? Is Jare ok?" I asked as I took a seat beside Paris and ran my fingers through her long pretty hair. In all my years of being with King, I had never seen that man shed a tear.

"Don't touch me"," she said as she jerked her head away from me. "You have put everybody's life in danger because you decide to have a sneaky pussy. Because of you, Jare is laid up in the hospital." I stood up, and slapped Paris across her face. It didn't matter what I did, she would respect me as her mother.

"I am your mother, and you will speak to me with respect!"

"Nah, Latrice, she ain't gotta respect you on no level. You lost that respect when you cost me my money and drugs because you wanted to sneak around with my business partner."

Hearing him call me by my real name made my heart sink a little deeper than it already had. King had called me Queen since the day we met; he said it was the perfect name for the perfect rider. From that day until this day, I hadn't heard my real name. Crazy thing I didn't even think Paris knew my real name.

"King, let's just get to the point. What is this all about, because I'm sure I'm not the only one with skeleton in their closet"," I said while getting shot daggers. I stood on ten by myself, though, so family or not, we can all air each other's business in this bitch. No matter how much I had grown since being with King, I was hood believe that.

"As a man that gets out here and provides for his family every day, the only thing that I expected from you was a home-cooked meal and loyalty. You never had to go out there and work because I made sure home was always taken care of. There are days, I 'didn't know if I was' coming home. But when I see you and Paris that made me realize how lucky I am to have made it in this cruel ass world. I sent Jare on a run for me because I couldn't make it. I was ready to off my own child because I thought he had stolen from me. But the whole time, he was fighting for his life." I noticed Paris with a shocked look while King's eyes began to water up. At that moment, I was feeling like this was more about Jare than me.

"Ali told me everything, Latrice, if you felt lonely, then why didn't you leave? I wasn't holding you captive in here; you could have gracefully bowed out of this marriage. Not only did you lie and cheat, but you knew what he did and was still by his side"," he said as he slid his phone across the table. It was a picture of me going in and leaving out the Four Seasons hotel. I had been caught and there was nothing left for me to say.

"Dino will drop you off at the Four Seasons!"

"I don't need anyone to drop me off, I will gladly get my belongings and leave as I came."

"That's the thing, you came with nothing, so you will leave with nothing. Your accounts are frozen, and your cards are canceled. You are no longer welcome on these grounds, and the only reason, I'm allowing you to live is because karma will teach you a bigger lesson."

Both Paris and King walked off, leaving me, standing in the dining room, looking like a lost puppy. At that moment, I was happy Roscoe had stolen their money, because I would still be living sweet. I would still live like a Queen because I had rightfully earned that name.

Dino dropped me off and hadn't even uttered a word to me. I knew he was loyal to King, so I didn't even trip when he didn't say anything to me. He dropped me off and quickly pulled away.

"Hey, Ms. Tolbert!" the receptionist said, calling me by my maiden name.

"What did you just call me?"

"Ms. Tolbert! "Your ex-husband told me to give you this and tell you thanks for leaving the bags where they could be found."

"Was he alone"?" Instead of her ghetto ass answering me, she took out a stack of cash and walked off with a smirk. Without saying anything, she had answered all of my questions.

My dear,

I told you that your karma would be much worse than killing you. I want you to see how it feels to live after betraying me. You living will be worse than a slow torturing death. I decided to take your play toy as well as my bags he thought was his. I'm sure you will find a way, I also decided to be nice and pay for a one-night stay.

With love,

King Malachi Lee

I walked to my room with the letter in my hand, reading it over and over again. I refused to stand here and allow anyone to see me cry. This is what happens when you betray a nigga like King, and I had brought this on myself. So, I would cry to myself. I had just fucked myself with no vaseline and this was just the beginning.

16

King

Before I was some thug ass nigga, I was a man with pride, and never in my forty-six years on Earth had I ever been so hurt. However, my wife changed that in a matter of minutes. She added more fuel to a fire that I already had brewing. I would never just leave her ass out, but I would have to teach her a lesson.

You can't bite that hand that feeds you and Latrice had done that times ten. She knows how far my reach is and still decided to play on my top. I could have killed her as she stood in the foyer of our house, or even when she walked out that hotel. But for the sake of the love that I had for her and our child, I allowed her to live to see another day.

After being with a person for so long you start to notice the change within them. Her mood was different whenever I was around, her pussy gripped differently. Her body no longer screamed out for my touch. Over the years, I had been betrayed by some of the closest people to me. But I never expected my wife to do the same, she was my sanctuary. However, the feelings weren't mutual.

"King, it's been two days and Roscoe's still sitting in the warehouse stanking."

"Kill him!" was all I offered to Meech. Jare was still in the hospital, recovering; we had lost Gus again, and I was recovering from a broken heart. I was now worn down, and the street nigga in me had died.

Revealing that Jare was really my son was never apart of the plan. I had planned on taking that to my grave with me, but him being shot hurt me down to my core. We had a good relationship, and I felt telling him the truth would make him think I abandoned him when that wasn't the case at all. His mother felt it was best I stayed out his life if I couldn't marry her. I tried my best, but I didn't even know Bonnie had died until Jare told us his story about how he started selling dope.

"Dad, I know it hurts, but you lying here will only make it worse."

"You know what's funny, I met your mom is the Haynes Projects as well. I had been on the bock hustling since I was eleven. Taking care of my younger siblings, so the state didn't split us up was hard on me. That day, I met your mother, I had just turned eighteen—she looked young. But she was the prettiest girl I had ever seen. We began out as friends, making Jare's mother pissed, but she was just a fling, and I had never felt a way about anybody before. No matter what, though, I had never chosen an enemy over home."

The amount of pain she caused me didn't add up to my mama leaving me to raise all my younger siblings on my own. Imagine dropping out of school to keep food on the table. Latrice came around and began to help as much as she could. But honestly, we were in the same boat. That day, I met her, she had become my Queen, my backbone, my rider.

"Whew, this is too much for me to handle"." I laughed at Paris because she was dramatic just like her mother. "Are you going to tell Jare?"

"When the time is right"," I truthfully spoke.

I got up from where I was seated and stood in front of Paris, kneeling down on one knee.

"You will always be my princess, and I know me hiding the fact that Jare was your brother from you would hurt. But I had no intentions on hurting anyone, I did it to protect his feelings as well as yours. Me not being in his life was not my idea, but the fact that I wanted to be with your mother hurt his, and she decided to take him and run away."

Paris reached out and hugged me. In my eyes, I didn't care how old Paris was, she would always be my Princess. I know she loved her mother, but I also knew she looked to us as being a power couple, so witnessing the betrayal was harder on her than me.

"I love you, Dad. Now take a shower or something you starting to stank." I laughed and went upstairs to jump in the shower.

Thirty minutes later, I was dressed and heading out the door. I needed to go check on a few traps, get a fresh cut, and go to the hospital to see Jare. Soon, I would tell him everything, because rightfully if I was to die everything, I had would go to him and Paris. But I didn't want him to find out after my death.

17

Paris

This damn family was just full of all kinds of surprises. I found out my mother betrayed the family trust, and that Jare was my brother all in the same day, that shit was crazy. But despite my mama betraying us, I refused to have her out here homeless. The Haynes was no place for a woman like her to live. I had no problem using my card to put her up in a hotel for an extra month. King was going to come around soon.

After waiting for about forty-five minutes, at her favorite restaurant Cheesecake Factory, I was starting to think that she wasn't going to show up. But it was like her to be fashionable late.

"I started to think you wouldn't show"," I said as she took a seat across from me. I remembered my mother being so beautiful, but these days she was lost. Her and King were a force to be reckoned with and without each other, they were both lost.

"I almost didn't because I don't need you throwing anything in my face. I already feel bad enough about this damn drama I've caused."

"I'm not here to judge you. I just want to know why you did it. Did you not love him anymore?"

I hated to put her on the spot, but I needed to know where her head was. My mother had always held everything down around the house. She would always be smiling while listening to her blues, so I wanted to know at what point did she become unhappy. I have never seen my father so hurt before.

"Girl, I have loved your dad since I first laid eyes on him in Haynes projects. But the thing you will learn is dealing with a man like King and Meech is the many lonely nights. You just don't get use to them; you won't ever get used to the many different hoes playing on your phone all hours of the night. The fake pregnancies, I lost count of how many bitches I've killed, or beat the fuck out of because of your dad. If I hurt your father, it was never my intention because I didn't plan on getting caught. But Roscoe showed me love your dad long ago, stopped showing. The thrill of feeling like someone loved me again was all I needed. It gets lonely at the top and no money or gifts can fill that emptiness that your heart holds. I know I started a war, but, at the end of the day, I will protect the both of you."

She was right about one thing, if nothing at all it does get lonely at the top and somedays, I started to hate it. I had my own money because of who my father was, but I still needed and wanted my man. I missed his touch and our late-night talks. Something wasn't sitting right with my spirit, but for now, I wouldn't speak on it.

"I see you over there thinking about what I said but don't overthink it. That alone will drive you up a fucking wall, I'm telling you firsthand. That's what got me in the situation I'm in right now, instead of just leaving. I measured arms with my husband, and I lost myself."

I stood from where I was seated and walked around the table to where she was seated. Love was a crazy thing and had a way of bringing the worse out of people. But betraying someone close to you is equivalent to someone physically stabbing you in your heart. The shit hurts like a muthafucka."

"Stop crying, Ma! I just wanted to let you know, I extended your stay at the hotel."

"Get your money back, or you can go enjoy and get your mind off things. I went back to Madea for the time being."

As much as my mother claimed she hated being in the projects, I know she slicked loved that shit. We all had a little of it in us and no matter how many times we left; we always found our way back there.

"Whatever makes you comfortable. I brought some of your clothes with me too."

"Thank God because I got tired of wearing your grandmother's duster. Lord, knows me and that lady don't have the same style."

"You know I'm sorry for the way I spoke to you, right?"

Silence fell upon us and we just got up and embraced one another. No matter what my mother had done, I was hurting for her the same way I was hurting for my father. If not the same, worse because all she wanted was love. I had no doubt in my mind that we would soon be a family again.

━━

"WHERE HAVE YOU BEEN?" I thought about what my mother had said earlier. Even the part about overthinking

73

myself, but Meech was constantly ignoring my phone calls was getting out of hand.

"Working!"

"You sure about that? Because it's going on four in the morning, and last I checked you were the boss and not a worker."

Meech just sighed and went to the shower. I wanted to stay in bed and remain calm, but something in me wasn't sitting right. I jumped out of bed and followed him into the bathroom. Before I spoke, I stood by the door. taking in his body, noticing the many scratches among his back. The blonde strands of hair mixed in with his dreads, and the red lipstick on the waist of his briefs.

"Why you staring at me like something on your mind?"

"Just decided to come and apologize and got stuck admiring your body." The smirk that graced my face was more of an evil one, instead of a sweet one. Meech had crossed a line with me and there would be no coming back this time.

"Join me!"

"Nah, love that's all you." Niggas were slap bullshit. How did you ask me to join you in the shower after fucking on another bitch? I turned to walk away, but not before grabbing his phone that sat on the counter. Never in my life have I ever gone through a man's phone, but things were about to be different.

18

Meech

"Girl, yes, he telling this hoe he loves her, and want to have kids with her"," Paris said into the phone while scrolling through my text messages. I knew she was on the phone with no one other than Cassidy.

"He was even on the side of me, in bed, sending some of these texts." I grabbed my phone out her hand and watched as she began to laugh.

"Let me call you back, Cass."

I was stuck without anything to say because I was caught. But Paris's nutty ass was scaring me because she was so quiet when usually she would have so much to say. Instead of addressing the situation, she walked into the closet and began to get dressed.

"Can we talk about this?"

"When I make it back, be gone"." She walked out of the room, leaving me stuck. Paris was the sweetest part of my life, and I felt safe with her. But I was tired of all the nagging and being tied down to one pussy was getting old.

Paris wasn't slick, though, I got dressed in a Nike sweat-suit and followed behind her. I put a tracker on her car a while back when Gus was still around. She wasn't that damn smart.

'Fuck,' I thought as I walked outside and noticed my car was gone instead.

It was damn near five in the morning and not many cars were on the highway, and I flowed through the city. I headed straight for Haynes Projects because I knew that's where I would be able to find Paris. My thoughts were beating me up because everything Paris read that I had sent Koti, I had been dealing with her for a while, and she held me down while I was locked up.

I promised Koti a life together, but when I ran into Paris all of that changed. I loved Paris, but I loved Koti too. After everything she had done for me, I couldn't just turn my back on her. Paris finding out this way was never my intention, but now since she knew, I knew I would have to make a decision.

In some way or another, they both had made a huge impact on my life. I could talk to Paris about anything because she was one of the homies. She had been through hell and back, but she prided herself on keeping her head up. She was rich and spoiled, but at heart, she was a hustler and that's what I like most about her.

Koti, on the other hand, had been taking care of herself all her life, so she was forced to get it out the mud. She never complained, always had a meal cooked for a nigga, and ready to suck my dick after a hard day of hustling. She was no better than Paris, but she was calm, and she was my getaway.

Pulling up in the Haynes, I noticed my car, so I headed straight for Koti's place. I didn't even kill the car, I kept it running and ran straight for Koti's crib. The moment, I reached her door, I heard screaming and arguing. I felt less than a man at that point.

"Paris, just let me explain"," I said as I pushed the door open. I don't know what had snapped in her head, but she was looking like a madwoman. The way her hair was curly over her head and her eyes were red, I knew she had been crying.

"Explain!" Her gun was cocked and aimed at Koti. I stood between the two of them and noticed how hurt she was.

"This isn't Koti's fault and everything you read today is true. I do love her, but I also love you, too. I would be a sucker ass nigga if I allow you to kill her, knowing I have feelings for her."

"You're right, Meech, I won't kill you or her. I lost myself in a man before, and I refuse to do it again. Any man that stands in front a gun for a woman obviously loves her more than he loves himself."

"Paris, as a woman 'I'm sorry, I know your pain, and I can relate"," Koti said, trying to smooth things over.

"Girl, you don't know my pain and you can't relate to a muthafucking thing. Until you stand in your nigga's side bitch house, holding a gun to her while he blocks the bullet, then we can never relate. Fuck all that girl power bullshit and fuck y'all too."

Paris lowered her gun and placed it behind her back before leaving without saying another word. My heart ached for her but what sense would it make to go running behind her after what I had just said. Once it was just Koti and I alone, I grabbed her and pulled her in for a hug.

"Will she kill me?"

"No, 'I'm here to protect you; go pack your bags. You'll be moving in with me."

After being in jail for so long, I was confused and all I was worried about was catching up on some pussy. I'm sure I would pay for this later, but I had options.

⊂⊃

"THE FUCK you think King called this mandatory meeting for?" Jare asked. He had to use crutches to get around, but he was doing much better.

We were all sitting around the table were we did our monthly meeting, waiting on King to come in the room. These last twenty-four hours of my life had been hectic, and I wasn't in the mood to be here right now. Even though I made the decision to be with Koti, I couldn't help but think about Paris. I reached out to her, but she had me blocked.

All I wanted to do was apologize being that I had to work on the side of King. I didn't want things to be awkward before I fully took my seat as head of the cartel. But I knew Paris would not make this easy for me.

19

Paris

After Meech decided to play with my heart, I decided to play with his pockets. Bitch, you would die of starvation before you eat on these streets ever again. I'm the daughter of King Malachi and since Jare has yet to know King is his father, then that throne Meech wanted so badly was rightfully mine.

"You sure about this?"

"Yes, Dad!"

My reach was entirely too far to let a pussy nigga play on my top. I called the Diego, Colonial, and Rosier family, demanding them to cut all ties with Meech. They wouldn't do anything to piss my father off, so they all agreed. Meech was now an enemy of the Lee family.

Walking through the warehouse with my family by my side felt powerful. The only thing that could be heard was my heels clicking across the floor as I walked to take a seat at the head of the table. Making eye contact with Meech, I gave him a quick smirk, then turned my attention to my father.

"Thanks for coming on such short notice. For those of

you that didn't know I had a daughter, well, I do, and as my child she is the only heir of my operation. A few weeks ago, Meech was to take over, but being that there has been some craziness going on Paris will be stepping up as I step down. I know a lot of you may not like that, but the bottom line is, she's my daughter, and I will kill anyone of you niggas that disrespect her."

I didn't want to run no damn cartel, I just wanted to show Meech I could fuck with him the same way he fucked with me. Only I could do it worse, so all the mugs can be saved because King would still run things. I had no interest in none of this shit.

"I'm sure quite a few of you are pissed at the decision my father has made. But no need to be mad because things will still run the same way they've been running. Nothing is to be done differently. However, my father and I just got off the phone with some very important people and we have all decided to cut Meech out."

"What the fuck!" Meech jumped up and screamed, and I noticed how pissed he was, and I couldn't help but laugh. "You can't do that, Paris!"

"Oh, but I can, and I did. Jarcole, you are cut off from the Lee family as well as everyone else. Dino will see you out, and you are no longer allowed in our headquarters, or any other property owned by the Lee family. You are dismissed!"

I looked in his direction and watched as Jare stood behind him and followed him out. Jare was loyal, so he did as he should. Either this would teach Meech a lesson or create a war. Whichever he decided to do, the choice was his. My job here was done. I walked out and let my father take over. Meech needed to hurt the same way I was hurting.

20

Cassidy

I was beyond pissed at Paris. I was even more pissed that Jare was up and walking around, instead of resting like the doctor said. Grant you, I understood Paris was hurt. But she went too damn far with the stunt she had pulled. The shit was bitter, and she knew Meech busted his head to sit at the head of that table. For her to cut him off, and tell the other connects not to deal with him was fucked up.

"I swear I'll fuck that bitch up on sight!" I looked at Koti and rolled my eyes because she had nothing to do with this.

"Nah, bae, I don't want you to get involved. I already put you in a crazy position, and I don't want to bring you into any more drama."

"This what got you cut off in the first place." Seeing Paris stand in my doorway was surprising. I knew it would be some shit today, I had a gut feeling. But then again, it could be the movement of the baby.

"I came by to drop a few of your things off, Cassidy. I noticed you packed up, so I figured you needed some help."

"I was going to call you later, and talk about everything with you. But I can't stay there knowing you cut Jare and Meech off. My loyalty is to them, P."

"No need to explain, love. I understand, but you need to learn to stay in your place when it comes to this business. Jare could never be cut out of anything, because he is the rightful heir to everything King Malachi owns."

"What you talking about, Paris?" I looked from Paris to Jare to see what the fuck was going on.

"Jare is my brother, King is his father. He's more than welcome to come back whenever he's ready."

Meech being pissed didn't faze her not one bit. She was hurt and was around here cutting people off and just airing business out. She was hurt, and I could see the pain in her eyes through her dark shades. I felt for her, but I stood behind my cousin and my man.

"The fuck you acting like this for? You know I'm the mind behind the business. You cut me out because you mad, I didn't choose you. I never meant to hurt you, but my heart was no longer with you. You a spoiled little bitch and it shows."

"Chill, Meech, she's been through"—"

"Girl, I don't need you to have my back," she said, cutting me off.

"I don't have your back, I actually feel sorry for you."

Paris looked at me and removed her glasses. Her eyes were so full of hate, and I knew her heart equally matched. This was the end of our friendship and for me it would hurt. But I knew it was no coming back.

21

Paris

I wasn't about to respond to Cassidy because I already knew the bitch was a snake. Her choosing her cousin after everything I had done for her was no surprise. She needed to just mind her fucking business before I applied pressure to her. You eventually learn your real friends from the fake ones. Cassidy was a foe because whatever chance she got, she moved like a snake.

I really loved her like a sister, but you had to watch out for a bitch like her. I threw my shades back on and walked out the same way I went in. Everybody in that apartment would be put behind me. Hopefully, one day, Jare and I could have a sister-brother relationship, but if not, that was fine too. Once the door closed behind me, there would be no looking back.

My ride home, I started to think about the crazy year I had. Dealing with Gus, then Meech, fake friendships, finding out Jare was my brother, and then add my parents splitting up, it had all become too much for me. At this point, I was over it and cutting Meech off was out of my character because I was more of the humble type. The revenge game was not for me.

Loving someone and being hurt over and over again was for the birds. I wanted to be at peace with everything around me. Baton Rouge was becoming too much for me. Nothing was here besides bad memories.

"How do you feel about that shot you called earlier?" my father asked once I walked in the house.

"Not good!"

"I figured you wouldn't and that's why I just got off the phone with Meech. He understood, but I was pissed to find out you went behind my back and told Jare, he was my son. You out here acting on emotions, Paris, that shit is only going to hurt you in the end."

"I'm sorry. I never meant for any of this to happen, but on the way over, I was thinking. I think moving away for a while and opening up a shop somewhere else is what I need."

"Maybe you should take a break from here for a while. You have dealt with too much, and the way you are going about it is wrong. Now, I have to go holla at Jare and Meech."

"Maybe you should go holla at mom, too."

"When the time is right, I will!"

For the first time in a long time, I had disappointed my father, and that alone had me feeling like I fucked up. It was really time for me to get the fuck away from here, and learn to love myself a little more before loving someone else. I would book a flight to Miami tomorrow morning, and start my new life there.

22

Three Years Later

"Stay away from that pool, Prince."

I was out in Miami, sitting poolside with my son, Prince and my friend, Dior. Yes, you heard right, I have a child. God always had a crazy way of healing broken hearts. He was the best thing that had happened to me. About two weeks after, I moved away, I found out I was pregnant, but chose not to reach out to Meech. He and Koti were living a good life, and they had a child together. I didn't want to intervene with my problems.

Moving out here was the best thing that had ever happened to me. I had opened another boutique and business was great. Meeting Dior was a plus; she was a breath of fresh air, and since meeting her, I had yet to question her loyalty. She was the sister I wanted Cassidy to be.

"You still coming with me this weekend, right?" I asked Dior. This weekend my parents were having an anniversary party. It took some time for them to get back right, but they managed to pull through and come back together. They were stronger than they were before.

Jare had even forgiven my father and the three of us

had an unbreakable relationship. Queen was basically like a mother to him as well. We had become the perfect family, but Jare knew I wasn't fucking with his girl or Meech for that matter. Whenever he would call, he made sure not to mention them just like I kept Prince a secret from him.

"Hell, yes, I'm trying to get one of those boss ass niggas like you."

"Girl, please, my daddy is the boss ass nigga. I had money before Meech ass came around. That lifestyle ain't the one you want."

"Baby, you must not know my history." I looked at Dior and laughed at how serious her facial expression was. Come to think about it, I really didn't know much about Dior, besides the fact that she ain't really have shit. She never spoke on her parents or her past life. The day she came in looking for a job, we connected and since then, I helped her get on her feet.

"Are you going to tell him?"

"No, I will just let Madea watch him the night of the party just so he won't see him."

"What about that bitch Cassidy?"

A few times, Cassidy had reached out to me, but I blocked her and pushed her to the back of my mind. She and my brother were together which was fine by me. I just had nothing to do with her and that day, she played with my brother would be the end of her. I have been waiting to sing that bitch a lullaby.

"You ain't gotta answer just know I'm on whatever you on." One thing for sure, I knew Dior was indeed a certified stepper.

———

WE HAD FINALLY MADE it to Baton Rouge to celebrate

with my parents, and I was tired as fuck. I don't know why the fuck I chose to come into town the day of the damn party. Queen greeted me as soon as I stepped foot out the car, and we hugged for what seemed like forever. I missed my mother, she was my best friend, and we had done some crazy shit together.

"'I'm happy you made it. Where's Prince?'"

"I dropped him off by Madea since the party is literally in two hours."

I can see the sadness across her face, and I swear it felt like my mother came to visit us every other month just because she wanted to be with Prince. My dad's eyes weren't big enough for him. But they just didn't know I was leaving him down here for a few weeks, because mama needed a break.

"Dang, Paris, I ain't know you were living like this, girl. You have a house inside of a damn house."

Both King and I fell out laughing at Dior. She was very blunt and her personality could bring out the best in anyone. I thank God for sending her my way because she has helped me in ways she didn't even know. Depression was real and when I first moved, I was on my own. Like I said, though, God had a way of mending broken hearts.

"Choose a room, sis!"

I was in the room, getting ready for the party when I started thinking back on everything. I didn't know if it was a good idea being back here because things always went crazy whenever we were all in the room with one another. I hadn't seen Meech, Cassidy, or Koti in over three years, it was best that they stayed out my way.

Since the party was in the backyard, I chose a cute simple outfit. I had on some camouflage shorts, a white button-up shirt, leaving a few unbutton to show a little cleavage. I had just ordered a pair of Gucci tennis, so I decided to break them in. My bundles were custom colored and styled into a bob. I had to look in the mirror because I knew I was bad. But it wasn't a bitch alive that could touch me now.

"Damn, girl, how you late to a party at your own house?"

Dior had on an all-in-one jean jumper with a pair of Tory Burch slides and her hair was pulled up into a ponytail. She topped her look off with some diamond studs and some nude lip gloss. My girl was bad as fuck, and I reminded her every day. Niggas in Miami would throw themselves at her, but she wanted a drug dealer, though.

The closer I got to the back yard, the more nervous I was getting. Like I said, I hadn't seen half of these people in three years. I didn't know what the fuck to expect, but one thing for sure, though, I still didn't mind busting Bella at a bitch. I was happy Meech was up now, but I still hated him for the way things went down.

As soon as I opened the door to the backyard, the smell of barbecue and boiled food invaded my nostrils. It had been so long since I had some good southern food. I damn near left Dior standing by the door and rushed to where the food was, grabbing me a plate.

"I see some things don't change"," Dino said as I cut the whole line to eat. I couldn't help but laugh at him because I used to send him on plenty of late-night food runs for me. After grabbing everything I was going to eat, I went and took me a seat by the bar area. Looking back, I was happy to see Dior interacting with people because I was too busy feeding my face.

"You hungry, huh?" I thought I was in love the first time I laid eyes on Meech. But the man sitting on the side me was God's gift. I damn near choked on my food looking up at him.

"Sorry, if I scared you, but your friend told me you could use some company." I looked back and saw Dior looking my way with a big ass grin on my face. The nigga she was with was just as fine.

"It's cool my name is Paris!"

"Juice!" he said as he grabbed my hand and kissed the back of it.

"Why they call you that?"

"Because I got the juice, baby."

"Cocky, huh?"

"Where you from? 'I've never seen you around here before!"

"I'm from here, but I moved to Miami. I just got in town today."

Juice pulled up a seat and we began to talk more. I decided not to tell him who my father was. Even though it seemed like I had money, I wasn't in the mood for another nigga to use me to get in better with my father. You would get to know me first, then maybe I'll allow you to meet King.

I was enjoying myself with Juice and Dior we were throwing back drinks and clowning around. For the first time in three years, I had made eye contact with Meech and the feelings I thought were gone came running back at once. His dark skin was still so smooth, and he was looking like more money than before. I just turned my head and chose to pretend none of them existed.

"You know them?" Juice asked.

"Nah!"

"Oh, you must really not be from here. Well, the one with the dreads and diamond grill is Meech and that's his girl, Koti. That hoe strung out and a few of my niggas done flipped her. The one standing next to him is his righthand man, Jare, and his girl, Cassidy. This Jare pops party matter fact."

"What's good, baby sis!" Just as Juice finish rambling by the mouth, Jare walked over to me and pulled me in for a hug. The look on Juice's face was priceless while the one Dior's face was lust-filled. I couldn't help but laugh at the way Juice stood there looking at me.

23

Meech

"Come on, get your shit together and clean yourself up!"

I didn't know how much longer, I would be able to feel sorry for Koti, or how she even got strung out in the first place. She was once so pretty, but she decided drugs were bigger than her and her family. She laid around all day while our nanny, Nancy, had to do everything.

"I'm going to drop Riley off, so be ready when I come back."

We were already late for King's party, and I had to go all the way across town to drop Riley off by Queen's mother. It was crazy that she refused to move out of Haynes Projects no matter how much Queen offered her. But I appreciated her and Queen for helping me because Nancy needed the weekend off. I was starting to think this was my karma for the way I had done Paris.

When I pulled up to the projects, I grabbed Riley and walked straight toward Madea's crib. I was so happy to see her sitting outside because I needed to drop her off and go.

"Whose baby you holding?" I asked as I sat my baby down beside her.

"This Paris boy, she came in town for her parents' party today."

"Oh ok!" I just stood there and stared at the kid before walking away. He looked so much like me, but I knew he couldn't be from me. No one had even mentioned a child to me. Jare is always talking to her, and he hadn't said anything either.

I was shocked to know that she was in town because she basically went ghost. Jare talked to her, but claimed he didn't know where she was living. I guess he had chosen to make sure his sister was happy over Cassidy. Deep down, I knew he was still there because of the kid because since he found out that King was his pops, he had really come all the way up. Hell, we both had.

Cassidy had tried to reach out to Paris a few times within the first two years. But she wasn't fucking with her at all, and I didn't even blame her. Cassidy should've just played her part, and stayed in her place. Instead, she wanted to act like the big bad wolf. Which only had her looking stupid in the end because King and Queen hated her guts and made it known whenever she was around.

Finally, we all made it to the party, and everything was in full swing. I wish to someday be as happy as King and Queen. They had been through hell and back and from the outside you wouldn't even know.

"I'm about to go holla at Paris"," Jare said as he walked off and headed in her direction. She was most definitely living a good life, and she had picked up weight in all the right areas. The girl was pure beauty and a hustler, and I knew I had lost the best thing God had blessed me with.

Walking her way would never be a good idea, so I just chose to mingle with people. At one time, I admired Koti, and I felt I made the right decision. But maybe my judgment was being clouded, and I tried to draw away from loving on my boss's daughter. Paris was loyal and would have a nigga's back through whatever. She was a fighter and a shooter, and she didn't mind going to war with you. I was just tripping hard as fuck.

As the night went on and the party began to die down, it was just a few of us left. Jare was standing back, talking to Paris's friend, he just no longer gave a fuck, and I would just mind my business. P and Queen were picking up things off the ground, throwing them away while I was talking with King. Cassidy and Koti really looked as if they didn't belong out here.

"Excuse me!"

Paris said as she made her way by Cassidy to clean up the mess on the side of them. I focused my attention to them just to make sure nothing went down between the three of them.

"Hey, P, mind if we talk!" Cassidy desperately grabbed Paris around her arm to stop her from walking away. She had no friends and she didn't really fuck with Koti, so I knew she missed Paris. But like I told her, both me and Jare were grown, and she should've never gotten in our business. As bad as I wanted to go over there, I decided to stand back and watch the two of them.

"What's up?"

"Hey, I've tried to reach out to you a few times. Just wanted to let you know, I missed our friendship, and to tell you that I'm sorry." Cass's eyes watered but no tears fell.

I know it took a lot for her to say that, but Paris was just one of those chicks you didn't want to cross. She was gutta and lived by loyalty. Don't let that big ass house she came out of fool you. King had taught her the streets. She was no fucking dummy at all.

24

Paris

I looked down at Cassidy as she grabbed my arm. To be honest, I didn't care to hear no weak ass apology. This wasn't the first time she had put her nose in something dealing with Meech and I. I meant what I said the day I walk out of her spot. Cassidy was dead to me and it would be no coming back this time around.

"Girl, I came down here to celebrate my parent's anniversary, not mend no friendships. That last time was the last time"," I said as I looked at Koti and took in her deadly like appearance.

"P, you cut my cousin and Jare out because you were being bitter and you mad 'cause I felt some type of way."

"You keep saying I cut Jare out, but as you can see this is his damn operation. If King dies today or tomorrow, the seat at that table is rightfully his. He, just like myself, is the child of King Malachi. Jare left because he's loyal to Meech, but you know nothing about loyalty. You always jumping into something that has nothing to do with you. The day you caught him with Jaymi, Meech was pissed that I jumped in and he refused to jump in. I'm letting you live because of my niece and the fact that my brother is with you. But I'm letting you know now me killing you will never be a problem. This oneway ass friendship we had is dead. Don't touch me again","" I said through gritted teeth.

"You sound real angry, Paris","" Koti said.

"And you looking real cracked out, Koti. Meech did good with his choice; he chose a crackhead and a flipper."

This was why I wanted these hoes to leave me alone. I ain't come down here for no fucking drama. I was seconds away from killing both of these bitches.

"Koti's right, though, I just wanted to apologize for what happened. But I see you still bitter that Gus beat your ass every day, then my cousin decided to leave you. Pussy can't keep a nigga for nothing, hun!" she said followed by a laugh. "I been had your dad number, but I had much rather see you struggle and get the fuck beat out you than help."

"Damn, that was low","" Dior said as she stood beside me. Instead of answering her back, I chose to walk away. I made my mind up to kill Cassidy, but it would wait. No tears were shed, but lines were cross when she let those words slip from her mouth.

Dior knew nothing about me, and I chose to keep her out of the violent part of my life. She knew my brother, father, and baby daddy were drug dealers, but she didn't know I would kill a bitch without blinking. Cassidy had fucked up and even Koti was looking at her sideways when she said that. But since she thinks getting my ass beat was funny, then I would tell Jare her little secret. Before walking in the house, I turned to Jare and whispered in his ear.

The mug he wore on his face was evident of the pain he felt in his heart. Cassidy knew me and she knew my reach, she forgot I knew all her little secrets. I watched as Jare made his way over to her, slapping her, then choking her up. Her death was near and from the look on her face she knew it as well.

―――

LATER THAT NIGHT, I was sitting in the bed, looking at my baby as he slept. My son was the best thing to happen to me and the spitting image of his father. I was beginning to give up on myself and love, but then God stepped in and gave me a reason to grind harder. He gave me a purpose.

Light knocks were heard before my door swung open. Meech stood at the foot of my bed with a drunken look on his face and his dreads hung over his eyes.

"That's my seed?" he asked as he pointed to Prince. I nodded my head without verbally responding to him. Grabbing my baby tight, I kept my eyes focused on Meech. At one time, I trusted him with my life, but these days he was a snake in my eyes.

"How did we get here, Paris? Where did we go wrong?"

I turned the lamp on that sat on my nightstand. Meech was still as fine as the day I met him in Haynes Projects. But he wasn't the same man I fell in love with. He was hurting, stressed, and tired; he wore the look of defeat all over his face. Grabbing Prince from the bed, I took him in the room with Dior. It was now time Meech and I talked.

He was sitting on the end of the bed with his head in his hands. The room was quiet, but light sniffles could be heard. Meech was broken because since I've known him, I had never known him to cry. We both went wrong, but I guess it was now time to talk and admit our fuck ups to one another.

"You chose not to be with me, but it was my fault too. I

was hurt from a past relationship, and hadn't given myself enough time to heal."

Once again, the room grew silent, but this time, I positioned myself between his legs and wrapped my arms around his neck. I buried my face in his neck and cried for the first time since leaving three years ago. We both cried to be honest, I guess this was well overdue.

Meech picked me up and laid me on my back, pulling my panties to the side. I didn't know if this would be a good idea, but how could I stop him when my yoni was literally screaming this man's name. I propped up on my elbows and watched as he placed his head between my legs and began to feast on my kitty.

"Shhhhhhh…"" light moans escaped my mouth and tears began to stain my cheeks.

"I never stopped loving you," Meech said in between licks to my clitoris. I arched my back and formed my mouth in the shape of an 'O.' Chills shot through my body and my toes started to curl and my ankles began to crack.

"I cumming, baby!"

"Cum for me, then." I exploded and watched as he licked me clean, then inserted himself in me and covered my mouth with his.

"I'm sorry, P!"

I kissed him back and chose not to answer. I would be leaving tomorrow morning. Meech hurt me to my core when he chose another woman over me. For the longest, I felt like he had done something wrong. I enjoyed the ride as we made love all night, but in the morning, I would be gone and he would be a distant memory.

25

Meech

Last night, felt so right because I honestly hadn't been happy in a long time. It was just something about Paris that I missed so much. She was the missing part of my life, and I had taken her for granted. When I rolled over the next morning, she was gone, and on her pillow was a note.

Dear Meech,

Last night was nothing short of amazing. However, it's nowhere we can go from here. I had to think about where we went wrong in our relationship, and as bad as I want to place the blame on you, I can't. I so badly wanted you to be different from Gus and love you the way, I deserved to be love that, I drew a wage between us.

I never meant for any of this to happen, but I guess not loving myself caused all of this. No healing and moving on too fast hurt us more than it should have. I didn't reply back to your apology because you didn't owe me one. I'm the one that needed to say sorry. Timing is everything, and I rushed into loving you before learning to love myself after being battered and bruised for so long.

I just want you to know how sorry I am. Our son's name is Prince King Lee and he's two years old. He loves to play basketball and eat pizza. We left to head home this morning. You were peacefully sleeping, so I didn't want to wake you. Hopefully, one day, you'll come around and be apart of his life. He's an awesome kid!

    Love always,

    Paris Narcole Lee

HERE I WAS LAYING in Paris's parents' house, getting ready to do the walk of shame because she decided to leave without waking me. One thing for sure that was the best sleep I've had in a long time. I threw my clothes on and threw the letter in my back pocket. She touched me to my heart with her letter because as we spent time together, she had never showed a sign of weakness. She had a few insecurities, but never gave me an impression like the past was bothering her.

Grabbing my jewelry, I rushed out of the room. Good thing no one was home 'cause I did not feel like hearing Queen's mouth today. She voiced how much she hated Koti and my mind was all over the place, so today was not the day for her opinions. Koti was cool at first, but I don't know where we went wrong. While she decided to chase her high, I was out chasing money.

⬜

'You should've just let me have you, I could've made you so happy
But I don't don second chances
Everything that happened forever, I wish you happiness
Never do this again—'

I WAS DRIVING down the street, listening to Kevin Gates when my phone rung, and I noticed it was Jare.

"What's up, lil' brudda?" I said as I answered the phone.

"Where you at?" I knew something was up from the tone in his voice.

"Floating around!"

"Man, look, we need to shoot out to Miami. Ole girl who was with Paris, just called screaming and hollering in the phone. I couldn't make out what she was saying, but I think something happened to P."

Immediately, I hung up and called my accountant to book two tickets to Miami. My heart had sunk in my chest because once again, I felt like I had let her down. But this time, I would save her. I shot Jare a text, letting him know I had gotten the tickets and told him not to tell King. I wanted to be the one to save her.

'*Just my luck,*' I thought as I pulled up to the crib and noticed Koti's car parked outside. I didn't feel like hearing the bitch's mouth today.

I ran in the house and began packing a few things without looking her way. Koti was once so beautiful, but these days, her looks weren't very pleasing at all. The battle she was struggling with threw her a curveball in life that she couldn't handle. Her face had sunken in and she wasn't pretty anymore. We haven't slept together, or in the same bed in a whole year.

"Where you going?"

"Miami!"

"Going to that bitch's rescue, huh?" I didn't answer her, I just looked her way and noticed the smirk she wore on her face.

"Let me find out!" I said before walking out the door.

I didn't want to look at Koti like she was on some bull-shit, but at the end of the day, she was a crackhead, and they were always on bullshit. Her saying something like

100

that made me raise my brow. All I said was, I was going to Miami, no one knew where Paris lived. Jare kept every-thing about her a secret, he never spoke on her around any of us. So, Koti was looking like a fucking suspect to me right now.

26

Dior

I was pacing back and forth, waiting for Jare and Meech to get here. I had no idea what the fuck was going on. One minute, Paris and I were on the phone talking, then the next I heard her screaming for her damn life. After that, the line went dead, I stayed five minutes away from her, so it took no time for me to make it to her place. Paris stayed in a nice upscale condo, so I didn't understand how someone was able to get in and take her.

I was happy as hell she decided to let Prince stay with her mother for a few weeks because whoever did this probably would have taken the both of them. I didn't understand how people could beef with someone like Paris, she was such a sweet person. She knew nothing about me, but decided to befriend me.

I had read all of Mz. Lady P books, though, so I was starting to think Paris was just a message for either Meech or her father. I didn't even know where to start looking for clues. I sent Jare my location and was waiting for him and Meech to arrive.

"Damn, P, I wish you would have told you more about your life"," I said to myself out loud.

Thankfully, Jare and I exchanged numbers before we left Baton Rouge because had we not, I would've have known what to do. I didn't want to bother him so soon, but at the end of the day, he was her brother, and they knew more about her life than me.

"Dior!" I jumped at the sound of my name. Running downstairs, Meech and Jare stood in the living room, looking around.

"What the fuck happened?" Meech jumped in my face like I had something to do with it. That alone made me cry harder than I already was.

"I don't know. I stay a few blocks away from her, so that's how I made it here so fast. When we both made it to our places, we were on the phone clowning around, and I heard her talking to someone, then I started hearing her scream."

"Did she say anything?"

"All she kept saying was Gus, or Russ, I don't know, something like that. I couldn't really make out what she was saying because the line went dead."

"Gus!" Meech and Jare said at the same time

"Where's Prince?"

"He stayed back with Queen for a few weeks."

"Jare, put a bounty on that nigga's head, ASAP."

I looked at Jare as he walked away to place a few phone calls. These niggas were some true bosses, and they didn't play behind Paris. There was so much hurt in his eyes, but I didn't know the full story behind him and Paris. But I hoped that they would someday be able to make up.

"Do me a favor and call Paris's mom and let her know what's going on. Tell her to get Dino to get my daughter as well—I don't trust that bitch Koti,"" he said with his brow raised. All them bitches were snakes if you asked me, but then again, no one asked me.

I grabbed the phone and call Mama Queen like he asked; I hated to hear her cry on the phone. But she already knew what came with the game, so she quickly got right and started doing everything I said. Paris was a casualty or maybe this was her war. Whatever it was, I was about to go to war with them niggas and bring my friend back.

"Stay here in case somebody calls"," Jare said.

"Boy, you dumb if you think I'm staying here." I reached behind my back and grabbed my diamond-encrusted Glock, cocking it back. Paris had pieces of her past she hadn't told me about, and so did I. Growing up in Liberty City, Miami, was no fun and killing a muthafucka today would not be the first body I've caught. All I knew how to do is survive.

"Gangsta bitch, huh?" Jare asked as he smiled at me.

"Y'all can be in love later!"

27

Gus

When I got away from Meech and King, I tried my best to stay low key until God called me home or Satan. But fucking around with these bird brain bitches; my death was coming quicker than suspected. They had me follow Paris from the airport and kidnap her. I could've declined, but the price offered wouldn't allow me.

It had been twenty-four hours since taking Paris and Meech was out in Miami, making niggas suffer for some shit we had done. Everybody had to pay because no one knew where Paris could be.

"Stop daydreaming and come help us!"

It was crazy how this whole thing was Cassidy's idea. I had seen Paris around Miami, but chose to let her be free. When Cassidy called me, saying Paris told Jare the baby was his, she came up with a plan to kill Paris. The same night of the party, Cassidy flew out to Miami and started putting her plan into motion.

She was jealous of Paris, and I didn't understand why, she was a beautiful person as well. She just came up in the projects, but you can always break that stereotype. Jare was one of the richest niggas in Baton Rouge, and you were around here, trying to kill his sister for exposing a secret. Technically, Cassidy brought that beef on herself.

She had always been that way, though, she knew about Cola before anybody else did. The only reason she didn't stop that fight was because I was fucking her too. These hoes were seriously tore up, she would even tell me everything Paris had said about me. Envy was a muthafucka.

"Let's just bring her ass back," I said while looking at both Cassidy and Tosha. These bitches were truly bat shit crazy.

"Let me find out big bad Gus scared."

"Didn't you say Koti called and said Meech caught a flight to Miami?"

"Yeah, and?"

"Bodies are fucking dropping in the city left and right"."

"Look, I'll return her after, I have a little fun with her"," Cassidy said.

Cassidy pulled Paris pants down and positioned herself between her legs. This bitch was most definitely on some stupid ass fantasy. But why not just ask, instead of raping the damn girl.

"Both of y'all bitches crazy."

Just as I said that. Paris started to stir out of her sleep. She began to look around and try to move her arms and legs. They had the girl tied to the bed and her mouth was taped shut, so her screams were unheard. No matter what I had done to Paris, I couldn't stand by and watch her cry in misery from her best friend. I turned to walk away, but not before making eye contact one last time.

"HERE DRINK THIS, and if you scream, they will finish you off." Tears threaten to fall, but she quickly blinked them away. As much as I hated Paris, I couldn't stand to see her like this.

"They slashed my face and cut my hair off." I took in her appearance and just that quickly she no longer looked the same. Apart of me wanted to reach out to Meech, but I knew calling him would be suicide.

"Why are y'all doing this to me? What did I do that was so bad?" I quickly covered her mouth and left out the house. She hadn't done anything to me, and that's why I felt so bad. These bitches were crazy, and I wanted no parts of it. I grabbed my phone, downloading a text free app, and prayed Meech still had the same number

Text free number: 5248 Cambridge Dr. Miami, Florida

I sent the address and disappeared into the night air. I'll lay up with my new bitch until the area was clear, but I didn't want to be around for what Meech and Jare brought.

28

Cassidy

Begin nice to bitches like Paris was unlikely. I didn't understand how she would leave a fucking mansion to stay in the projects. At that moment, I felt as if she was making fun of us for not having nowhere else to go. That was an insult to me when I saw her home for the first time. On top of all that, she was one of the most beautiful women that I had ever seen.

Every nigga wanted her, and I wanted to see what it was about her that made them go so crazy. I had to taste her because, despite both Meech and Gus leaving her, them niggas loved the fuck out of Paris. When I first licked her bottom lips, she had the freshest smell and taste like a Sunday meal. Maybe I would keep her around longer and continue to play with her.

"Get the fuck up!" I jumped out the bed at the sound of a gun cocking back. I knew Meech's voice from anywhere. He had that type of voice that would make the room shake, and right now he had me scared shitless.

"Where that nigga Gus?"

"Son, if you are going to kill me, then just do it because

I am not in the mood to talk." Meech looked at me with hurt and confusion in his eyes.

"I found her!" Jare said as he walked in the room with Paris's friend following behind him. He looked so confused when he saw me on the other side of the gun. Tosha stood in the corner naked, shaking like a leaf, as she begged for her life.

"Damn, Cass, I knew you had a few loose screws, but I ain't know you were this fucked up. The fuck you slashed my sister's face for?" Meech had jumped in my face ready to end me.

"Bitch, you cut my girl's face?"

"Is Jr from me?"

"No, he's from Gus!"

"Damn, bitch, you really ruthless as fuck. What has she ever done to you besides be your friend"?" This bitch had only been around for two seconds, but she knew nothing about my life.

This speech was starting to get old. Just a few months ago, he claimed he didn't even want Paris anymore. He was standing here, telling me about loyalty, but he been turned his back on her. I sat down on the bed because this was real hypocritical. Everybody in this room, except Dior, had betrayed Paris and she might do it next.

"Man, let me rock these hoes"," I heard Dior say.

"I'll tell you whatever you want to know, Meech, just please don't kill me. We have a child together."

"Tosha, shut the fuck up. You didn't think about her when you left her with your mother to come up here and kidnap people. Besides you know damn well that ain't my kid."

"Tosha, don't beg these niggas for your life. As I can recall, a few years back, Meech turned his back on Paris too. He walked away from her, then chose a crackhead whore over her. By the way, since we talking about kids, did you test Rylie 'cause I heard she from Ray Ray'"," I said, referring to a rumor, I had heard back home. "You know damn well, I ain't about to beg you for my life, I got too much pride for that, big cuz."

"'I'm telling you, Meech, let me rock this hoe for y'all.'"

Jare stood beside Meech with a cold look on his face, and I knew then he wanted to kill me. But the cat was out the bag, and he and I haven't had sex in over eight months, so I had started back fucking around with Gus. When he thought I was out on business, I was in Miami fucking and sucking on Gus. I knew who my child's father was from the jump, and the only reason I hid it was because I didn't want to hurt Paris's feelings.

I watched as Meech raised his gun and shot Tosha between her eyes. Her body instantly dropped, and I knew I was next. But I didn't care, I had been ready to meet my fate.

"It would hurt our grandmother too much if I kill you. But if you even cross my path again just know I won't think about her feelings." A sign of relief came over me, but before leaving he instructed Dior to beat my ass.

Out of all the dirty shit I've done, you would at least think I knew how to fight back. But I was no match for her once the first lick connected, I was out like a light switch.

———

MY BODY FELT like a ton of bricks were weighing on me. My eyes were swollen a little, but when I opened them, I noticed Jare in the corner of the room I was in. The beeping noises around me made me aware that I was in a hospital room. I was amazed to see him here by my side after everything I had done.

"Surprised to see you here," I sarcastically said.

"I came to finish you off since Meech couldn't do it because of y'all being family. But I had no relation to you, and the day you fucked over my sister, you instantly became a fucking memory."

"What happened to your arm?" I asked, noticing the cotton ball and tape that was in the middle of his arm. I purposely ignored what he was talking about because if he wanted to finish me off, I would be dead. It was just that simple that nigga loved me.

"Cassidy, I should've left your ass in the projects where I found you. But earlier that day, of the block party, I ran into Paris at the store and she vouched for you. She said you were different. She said you would be my peace when I felt the world was against me. She said you would be my rider and protect me when the streets got hectic." He had a look so evil and for the first time, since I had betrayed everyone tears stung my face.

"Before you kill me just tell Meech, I'm sorry, and Koti was the one paid us to do it."

"I'm not going to kill you, Cassidy. The karma you are about to go through will be far worse than what you've done to anyone. He that reason, I'll let you live your life"," he said, then walked out of the room, leaving me alone in deep thought. I just shrugged him off and wiped my tears away. I didn't need him or anyone else for that matter.

"Hey, Ms. Smith, I'm here to change your band around your arm to a new one."

"Red? What the fuck going on?"

"I guess your friend didn't tell you like he said he would. Well, when you came in your friend instructed us to run tests on both of you. Your results came back you were positive for AIDS."

"He gave me AIDS and left like it was funny. I swear I'm going to kill that bitch when I get out of here."

"Calm down, ma'am. Actually, your friend's results came back negative while you were positive. Its really no more I can tell you at this point, but we will have a specialist come in and talk to you about everything. Don't let this be the end of you, Ms. Smith."

She quickly changed my band and left the room. I knew something bad would come out of this because I had made too many negotiations with God and constantly did the same thing over and over again. I laid back in bed and balled up in a knot and cried to myself.

"My God! MY God!" was all I could say.

29

Paris

"What the price is, and I'll pay it, doc."

"I understand that, Mr. Lee. However, this has to be Paris's decision on whether she wants the surgery or not."

After going from surgeon to surgeon, my father and I flew out to Dubai to meet one of his friends that happened to be a doctor. I never knew someone could hate a person so much, but I guess I thought wrong. Everybody around me felt the scar wasn't that bad. My own insecurities would allow me to live with it for the rest of my life, though.

"I want it!"

The day Meech carried me out that house, he brought me to my parents, and I hadn't heard from him since. I knew it was because he took pride in my beauty, it was everything to him. The crazy thing is I learned long time ago there was no place in this world for Meech and I to live happily ever after. He was confused between two women, and I wasn't about to sit around and wait until he made his mind up.

My dad looked my way with hurt in his eyes. I knew losing me would be the worse thing ever, but I wasn't going anywhere anytime soon. Cassidy didn't really want to kill me; the dumb bitch just had her own fantasy she wanted to live. Chills ran down my spine just thinking about how sick the bitch was.

However, her contracting AIDS was a harsh punishment that I wished on no one. Gus had disappeared again. I was shocked hearing everything Paris had revealed. But after what she had done, I put nothing past her.

"I got you, baby girl!"

"I know!"

I hated that somebody I allowed in my home and trusted with my life had done me so wrong. Queen wanted the hoe dead and King wanted to kill Meech for letting her live. But at the end of the day, they were family, so I could only respect his decision. All his grandmother had was him and Cassidy.

Lately, I had been keeping my distance from Dior, she had come back to Baton Rouge and was getting close to Jare. We were all living under one roof and even though she hadn't done me anything. I was scared to trust anyone right now. Dior was nothing like Cassidy ass, I even heard how she knocked the bitch out behind me, but my trust was fucked up bad.

"If you want, we can set your surgery up for next week, and I can fly into town and do it at my office back home."

"That's cool!"

I was back to feeling how I felt when I was with Gus. It took me a while to walk with my head up again and smile the way I use to. The moment I was back to feeling like myself, it was taken away from me by somebody else I loved. The scar went from my ear to the middle of my cheek. Most days, I would get dressed in the dark because I hated to look in the mirror.

THE DAY of the surgery had finally come, and I was so excited to be back to my old self. I felt with this surgery, I would have a second chance at being pretty again. I wasn't worried about my hair because it always did grow back quick. It would be back down my back in no time. Hell, I kind of like the short look on me.

The door of the room swung open and Meech walked in holding Prince. I could see a future with him, but I know things aren't promising with the two of us. That didn't stop the fact that I didn't love him though.

"I wasn't going to let you go through this alone."

"Thought you had forgot about me!"

"Before you become out of it, its something I have to say to you." Meech grabbed my hand and took a seat beside the bed, placing Prince on his lap. In the perfect world this would be an ideal life. But in our world, there was too much drama.

"P, I know I haven't said much since the incident, but truthfully, I didn't know what to say. I never stopped loving you and the day, I let you walk out of Koti's apartment hunts me until this day. But I knew you would never forgive me for standing in front of that bullet for her, so instead, I allowed the best thing life has ever given me to walk away." Tears welled up in the corner of my eyes and began to fall at a rapid pace. Meech had never expressed his feelings like this before.

"Believe it or not, I have loved you since the day I laid eyes on you uptown. Without conversation, I could tell that you would bring nothing but good vibes my way. But I also know you had a story to tell because your eyes held so much pain. Even when you counted me out of your heart, you still ain't completely give up on a nigga. Paris Narcole

Lee, I took some time to think about the fuck-ups I've made in life and it's time to correct my wrongdoings. I love you with everything in me, you bring me peace, and when I'm with you I feel safe. I'm sorry for hurting you. Will you marry me?"

Just like that the damn anesthesia kicked in and my ass was out. Told y'all the universe just wasn't on our side.

30

Meech

I couldn't help but laugh to myself. Before Paris could respond to everything I had said, she was out of here. Now here I was sitting in the family room feeling about the decision I had made. Me not going around her since the incident was mainly because I felt like the shit was my fault. I had to square some things away before I went to get my girl back.

"You straight?" Jare hadn't said much since finding out about Cassidy. He just needed to be grateful he dodged a bullet.

"Shit, just a little fucked up about the shit. Never saw any of this coming. Even when I heard people say with more money comes problems, I just never thought it applied to us."

I sat back in my seat refusing to respond, but I took in everything Jare had just spoken. When I got out, I was promised a seat at the head of the King Malachi cartel. Which he came through with that promise. The only thing I wanted to do was make money and stay out the way.

Never in a million years did I think my own blood

would betray me because she was jealous. To make matters worse, she and Koti acted like they hated each other so much, but they were in together on kidnapping Paris. Koti must've gotten word that I was coming, and she packed up and left. Which was fine, I didn't want to kill the mother of my child.

I sent Jare to kill Cassidy because even though she had fucked up bad. I just didn't want her death to be on my hands, and we were all my grandmother had left. Finding out Cassidy had AIDS kind of surprised all of us, but Gus had been thinking she was cheating. She was always out of town doing this, but she was a stay at home mom. I don't know who the fuck she thought she was fooling, but the bitch ain't even have a job.

People outside looking in would've thought we were all some kind of power couple. In reality, we both stayed for the wrong reasons. I didn't want to see my kids calling another man dad and lil' brudda felt the same way. Instead of killing her, Jare felt her living with AIDS would be a better death sentence.

"Ms. Lee is requesting you, sir." An older nurse came up to me, and pulled me from my thoughts.

"How did everything go?"

"She's a champ and will be looking like her normal self in no time."

"Yes! Yes! Yes! I'll be your wife!"

Paris was screaming with excitement as if she hadn't just had an operation. However, I was happy to see how excited my girl was. We had been through so much since the day I met her, and through it all she stayed the same. I leaned down and kissed her on the forehead.

"Can't wait to get that pussy"," I whispered in her ear.

"I can't wait to ride your face."

"You think we gon' work this time, Meech?"

There was really no doubt in my mind that we wouldn't work out this time. It was still some things I had to get squared away, because I knew like hell, Koti ass wasn't just going to let shit ride. She would be back soon and the day she graced us would be the day, I have a bullet waiting for her.

Gus would get his day too, but I wasn't too focused on looking for him. Koti ain't come through with that bag since I froze all her accounts, so I knew they both would be coming by real soon. As bad as I wanted to marry Paris right now, I would wait until I got the beef handled. I didn't need nobody come fuck up nothing, I had going on this time.

"No doubt, ma!" I kissed her forehead again and walked out the room. One day, I inspired for us to be like King and Queen. They couldn't be fucked with when they were together. But apart they were weak, I no longer wanted to experience being away from Paris. Life wasn't the same without her.

31

Paris

The surgery went well and it was outpatient, so after resting a little while longer, the doctors gave me the ok to go home. The thing was that after Meech had proposed, I no longer knew where home was. Baton Rouge or Miami, and I didn't want us to get into over where we would grow old together because we had just gotten back cool.

Since the day I met Meech, I prayed he would make me his wife. There were days, I doubted the whole love thing because it was like when I gave my all. My all was never good enough, it was always something I wasn't doing right, and I was over the situation. But I had a damn good feeling about our future.

"Why are you acting funny with Dior?" Jare insisted on coming to pick me up and now I knew why.

"It's not that I'm purposely doing it, but I'm fucked up about how Cassidy played me. I knew she would do fake shit when me and Meech would be into it, but this was a different level. My mind fucked up bad."

"I know I may not know Dior all that well, but she seems like a real cool girl. This world we live in is fucked up, but it still has some people like us left out here. Fuck that hoe Cassidy, and don't push Dior away because I feel she got some shit she's dealing with as well."

Hearing Jare say that last sentence made me think back to when I first met Dior. She was always paranoid but kept a smile glued to her face, so I didn't think too deep into it. I would talk to her, though, because even though she was moving along good, I knew shit was far from over. I never told Meech that Gus was the one trying to help me.

I didn't know if I wanted to save him for trying to save me, or if I just felt sorry for him. One thing for sure, I knew saving him would be me being stupid because what he and Cassidy had done to me and my brother could never be forgiven. I wonder if she had gotten her AIDS from him, or if she was fucking with more than him. Thank God my brother and I are straight.

"I'll holla at her later, but get me home because my face is starting to hurt from the damn stitches."

Truthfully, I didn't feel like talking to anyone about anything they had going on. I know to some it may be self-ish, but I had some shit up my sleeve. Muthafuckas were about to feel me very fucking soon. But for now, I would just pop me a pain pill and cuddle with my baby.

32

Dior

Today had marked five years since the love of my life had died and my life had been in shambles since that very day. I locked myself away in the room and turned my phone off because I didn't want anyone to see this side of me. I was still in Baton Rouge for the time being, and we had all been staying with Paris's parents. The damn house was so big it was like we all had our own world. I understood that I needed to give Paris sometime to get over everything that had happened. But I would need all of their help soon.

"It cold out here, bae," my husband, Kole, said.

We were getting ready to go catch a movie and grab a bite to eat. I had just given birth to our baby girl, Chyna. She was so beautiful with a head full of hair and big bug eyes. Kole felt I needed a break from sitting in the house, but I had no problem being home. Because we were forever watching over our backs whenever we would be in the streets. That's the life that came with being a dope boy.

"We can always just grab a red box, and a bite to eat." I really didn't want to leave my baby with the nanny. I found her online and she had great reviews, but still in all, she wasn't me.

"No, bae, we are about to enjoy ourselves."

*I allowed him to open the passenger door and jumped inside,
turning the heat up higher. My body was shaking like a leaf as I took
the gloves off and rubbed my hands together in front of the vents.
Vibing through the streets of Chicago was cool, but I was missing
Miami like crazy. I just couldn't get use to the super cold weather.*

*Having my husband by my side was everything I had prayed for
as a child. We had more money than I had ever seen before in life. But
even with that money came problems. Kole was no saint, and he was
evil as fuck in the streets, but he was the sweetest man at home. But a
monster to those that would cross him.*

*We were at the red light, laughing and listening to music, when a
black Tahoe pulled up on the side of us. I paid no attention to what
was going on because I was just trying to enjoy the company of my
man. He got out the Tahoe and walked around to the driver's side of
our car and pulled Kole out.*

"Where the fuck is my money?"

*"I don't have it, Tone! Look, let me bring my girl home, then I
can meet you a little later." I guess he wasn't trying to hear that
because the next thing I heard was a gunshot and he walked away. I
waited until he pulled off to jump out the truck, and run around to
check on Kole. But when I made it over there, he had a single gunshot
to the head and his eyes were open.*

*"Damn, baby!" I grabbed my phone and called the police.
Staying until the whole scene was cleaned up, I got in the car and
went home. I knew the code of the streets, so I told the police the
person was masked. My heart had sunk until the chest and all I
wanted was my Chyna.*

*Pulling up home, I could see the living room light on, and the door
wide open. I ran in and blood was everywhere. But nobody was in the
house, I went from room to room. I screamed and cried because I had
lost the two most important people to me in the same fucking night.*

Unknown: Bring my money, bitch!

*Fuck Tone and his money, I wasn't bringing him shit. I mean
why would I? He killed my child and my fucking husband. I went*

into the closet and grabbed the bags of money Kole had ducked off
and loaded the car up. I had nothing to live for in Chicago anymore, so
I damn sure wasn't about to stay down here.

Knock!

Knock!

I quickly dried up my tears and went to answer the
door; I didn't want anyone to see me weak. But there were
days, I would sit and think about the two of them. I missed
them, and I should have fought harder, but I didn't. I just
left town only returning for the funeral. But I never went
inside the church. Chyna's body was never found, and all I
used to think was how could people be so damn ruthless
towards an innocent child?

"Why are your eyes so puffy and why you got the damn
door locked?" Jare said as he walked into the room.

"Just got a lot on my mind, feeling homesick."

"Dior, you know you safe with me, right? Whatever is
bothering you just let me know."

I knew I was safe here, but I didn't know if I could
really give Jare my all. I loved dope boys, but I only wanted
them around for sexual reasons only. Before meeting Jare, I
was able to do just that, but he was different. He always
made sure I was straight, and he noticed when I wasn't
balanced.

"Yeah, I know!" Today was worse than any other day
because seeing Prince and Riley run around here made me
miss Chyna even more. I wanted to see her grow up, I
wonder if she would look like me, or if she would look like
her father. I knew I would have to speak on everything
someday because the shit was affecting me badly. But I
knew they would look at me and judge me for not trying to
find out what happened to my baby.

"Dior, you sure you alright?"

"Yeah!"

"You keep checking out on me. Just know whatever the situation, I got you." Jare leaned in and kissed my lips. It was like lightning running through my veins when our lips connected. I knew then I had to tell him the truth about my life, but I felt that maybe running and not turning back would be better.

"Look, I gotta get out of here to go handle some business, but later, some very potential business partners are coming over. Get dressed up and join me tonight!" I nodded and kissed him before he left the room.

━━━

LATER THAT NIGHT, I was dressed in a beautiful floor-length, blush-colored maxi dress. I was shocked when Jare said Paris would be joining us because I knew how she felt about the bandage on her face. But my bitch was still beautiful and could out dress any bitch in the room.

Walking downstairs hand and hand with Jare felt amazing. I lived a good life with Kole, but this life here was better. Jare gave me the go-ahead to start looking for another crib for the two of us. But I wasn't too much feeling it because I felt we were kind of moving too damn fast.

"'Bout time you stopped crying and came out that room."

"Nah, Paris that was you shutting everybody off." We laughed and hugged each other as if we hadn't been living under the same roof for the past month.

While the men walked around mingling, Paris, Mama Queen, and myself were seated having our own side conversations. Other wives and girlfriends were there as well, but I hated that they were acting stuck up with all their diamonds on. I rolled my eyes and took a shot of my D'usse, I stood for where I was and went to go walk over to Jare when our eyes connected.

I dropped the glass where I stood shattering it all over the floor. My heart rate sped up and Paris came rushing to my side and tried to calm me down. This couldn't be happening to me, I was there. I saw him, I held him until the corner took him away.

"Kole!" I blurted out as he stood there on the side of the nanny that I hired with the devilish grin on his face. After I noticed the two of them together, everything went blank.

33

Kole

I'm starting to think that fucking over Dior ain't do shit, but backfire on my ass. Leaving her was not apart of the plan. However, it was the way things had to go. The nanny we hired real name was Karma and that bitch was really a pain in my fucking ass. But I felt I had to be with her to get further in life. Her family-owned cocoa farms in Jamaica, and it was simply all I had to do was find a way to leave Dior and take Chyna.

She wanted a kid, but couldn't have none, so I did just that. Tone was supposed to get the fucking money I had put up after he pretended to shoot me. But Dior got away when over two million dollars and never turned back. She didn't even file a missing person report on her daughter. She was thorough though, so I knew she knew what came with the game.

I hadn't seen her since that day, and I planned to keep it that way. I never meant to hurt her, so while I was living my life in Jamaica, I wanted her to do the same wherever she was. All I wanted was the money, so I chose to let her keep it for pain and suffering and live her life. But after moving to Jamaica, Karma's parents were killed, and King brought the cocoa farms out. That's what brought me to Baton Rouge, I had planned on doing business with him.

Seeing Dior brought back so many memories, but a part of me hated her for the way she was living, and I know it had nothing to do with my money. If she was in this house, then that meant that she was connected to some powerful people which meant she had money out the ass. I would have to stay around in Baton Rouge because she had something that belonged to me.

"Never thought I would see that bitch again?"

"What did she ever do to you?" I asked Karma, she hated the ground that Dior walked on, but it should be the other way around. Chyna was now four years old and she was the spitting image of her mother. It would be hard for me to look at her some time, because I could see the same pitiful look her mother wore the day, she thought I died.

"Why you always defending her? I hope you don't tell her the truth about Chyna because I will kill you if you try and take my baby from me."

Well, we would just have a damn shoot out because Karma didn't know that's exactly what I had planned to do. I don't know how bad she wanted her daughter, but I knew how much I wanted my money. I was going to offer her something she couldn't refuse; I was going to sell her daughter back to her for two million dollars. Either she would give me my money, or never get a second chance to be a mother to her daughter.

34

Paris

Something was really going on in Dior's life and she has had yet to come back out of that trance she's in. The child has been staring off into space since she came back from passing out. King dismissed everyone from his house, and now we were all sitting in the living room, waiting for her to say something.

"What is wrong with her?"

"I don't know. I walked in the room earlier and she was crying. Maybe it has something to do with that."

"Who was that guy?" I asked.

"That's Kole and his wife Karma. Karma is the daughter of the late Ska Marley; they owned a cocoa farm back in Jamaica but when Ska and his wife died. I offered his brother Silk $1.5 million dollars to buy the land and he didn't even think twice. I'm guessing they were here to either get it back or do business."

"Yeah, but what relations does he have to Dior"?" Look, this shit was starting to become too damn much for me. I was confused about the whole ordeal and was praying Dior wasn't on no snake shit like Cassidy. My camp couldn't take anymore betrayal.

"He's my husband!" Everyone stopped and looked back at Dior as tears rolled down her face. "But I was there when the coroner came and got him. I held his body as the blood from his face ran down my arms and legs. I don't understand and her"—" Dior jumped up like a madwoman and ran up the stairs.

I stood from where I was seated and went behind her with everybody following behind me. We were all looking at one another confused as fuck. Dior was on some crazy woman type shit, so whatever she had going on must have been something far more than we all thought.

"Dior, what's going on?"

"That bitch that was with him. I hired her as a nanny the night he was killed—she had good reviews. The website said she was one of the best, so I left and trusted her with my daughter. I had just given birth and he made me go out. When I returned home, the house was full of blood and she and my baby were both gone. I'm going to kill that bitch." Dior had already changed into all black and was placing her gun behind her back.

"You can't go out there alone!"

"I can, and I will. My baby might still be alive, Paris. I let them get away once, I won't let them get away again. If I gotta hunt them down and kill them myself, then I will do just that." Dior pushed passed me and got ready to walk out the door, but not before Jare grabbed her arm, and pulled her in for a hug.

Watching her break down had done something to me. As a mother, if something was to happen to my child, then I would be devastated too. I understood where she was coming from, but as her friend, I couldn't allow her to go out there on her own. She had no family and since meeting her, she had done nothing, but be loyal to me.

I walked out the room we were standing in and went to change into an all-black Nike sweatsuit with some black Air Max to match. These days my hair was short, so I threw on of Meech hats on and grabbed Bella.

"You ready?" Dior looked up with the biggest smile ever on her face. I didn't mind helping her out because to Meech's surprise this wouldn't be the last time I wear all black. I had a private investigator, watching all of Gus and Cassidy's moves. Sooner than later, I was going to kill the both of them.

"Oh, so, y'all just think y'all some gangsta bitches, huh?"

"Meech and Jare, go with these crazy-ass girls and Queen you don't even need to think about it."

"I never get to have fun anymore!" We all laughed at her pouting and headed out the house. Since I first picked up a gun and shot at someone the shit came easy. Before King moved us in a gated subdivision, we stayed a few blocks from Haynes. People often tested us, thinking my dad kept money or drugs in the house, so when they left to go on a date one night. Somebody broke in, but before they shot me, I had to get them.

The thing with being a kingpin's daughter is the game will be taught to you whether you chose that path or another. I graduated high school and could have gone to college too, but I was being dumb in love. I've done pickups for my father and even counted money so much, I was counting it in my sleep. I lived the life of a boss surrounded around bosses. King ain't raise no fucking fool, this shit came naturally. I got a rise out of killing people, but this may affect Dior.

"You know you don't have to do this if you aren't ready?"

"Girl, I've been on my own since I was fifteen, and all I know how to do is survive, and I'd be damn if y'all go find my baby, and I'm not there. I don't talk much about my past because it's called that for a reason, but please don't think I haven't killed before."

I wasn't used to this cocky Dior, but I liked her. I just gave her a head nod and threw my hands in the air. She was ready to play, then lets head the fuck up out here and handle business. While in the car, we all passed the blunt around, and went to the address King had on Kole.

King was supposed to originally meet Kole on his own, but had a change of heart for some reason. To me that reason was God giving Dior a second chance, but others might say it was King just being his bossy self, making Kole wait.

On the ride over, I could tell Dior's mind was every-where, except where it should be. I was wondering if we were thinking the same thing, like what if her daughter wasn't there and she didn't have another chance. I prayed that wasn't the case, though, I wanted to see her happy like she was when I had first met her.

"Grab that automatic out for me, bae," Meech said.

We were pulling up to the address King had provided. The house was weary as fuck and looked like a trap house. This had to be a fucking joke. How the fuck could you afford to score, but live in something like this?

"Y'all ready?" Jare asked, looking directly at Dior. "Follow my lead!"

Dior took off, walking in the direction of the house without looking behind her. She shot the doorknob off the door, and walked straight in.

"She's going to get us caught, get the crazy bitch,"

Meech yelled. At this point, I ain't even blame her. Had my child been involved, I would feel the same way.

"Let her air this bitch out until she finds what the fuck she's looking for." I shrugged my shoulders, and followed behind her.

This damn house was so cold and weary. I knew in my heart something wasn't right. It was like we were walking into our own trap. My gut feeling was telling me something was about to go down.

"I smell gas," 'both me and Meech spoke at the same time.

The house was clear, and by the time we turned around and made it out, the house exploded. Pain shot through my body and everything went numb. I could hear Meech calling my name, and I even felt him grabbing for my hands.

I should've left when my gut was telling me to. Either this nigga knew we were coming, or he had set this trap up for my father.

―⬛―

"I'LL HANDLE KOLE!" Dior said.

Thankfully, we were all out of the house and only caught the impact of the explosion. My arm was in a sling; I fractured it when I flew in the air. Everybody else was straight. I felt the damn heat radiating off King's body, so I knew he was pissed off. His thoughts were just like mine, Kole knew we were coming. He was trying to take my father out.

"Nah, we will handle him!" I nodded my head as Meech spoke. "You are in no shape to take on situations like this. Just sit back and we will bring baby girl back to you."

"I don't care what y'all say, I will handle this shit on my own. She's my daughter, and I let her go once, and I refuse to let her go again","" she said, trying to storm off, but not before I grabbed her by the arm.

"You will not handle a muthafucking thing. You ain't no fucking killer, you out here acting on emotions and could have gotten us all killed tonight. Like Meech said, we will handle this and bring her back. Hell, I'll even bring Kole and Karma to the warehouse and allow you to kill them. But you can't come out here acting the way you acting." She jerked her arm from me and ran up the stairs with tears running down her face.

"You cold, sis!"

Ding Dong!

"Grab the door, Dino."

Dino left and came back with Kole following behind him. Dior was doing all the crying and we ain't even have to go look for this nigga. He graced us with his presence.

"I'm not here on no war shit, I just want to speak with Dior."

"You sure about that being that you invited me over to your house to kill me."

"I ain't invite you nowhere!" Kole spoke with a mug.

"Yeah, well, somebody out her playing like you and about to get you murked. My girl sprained her fucking wrist because y'all wanted to do science projects."

"Man, look, I don't know about all that. Most times, Karma handles the business part of everything. I'm just here to holla at Dior about something before I head back to Jamaica."

The room grew silent as Jare ran upstairs to get Dior. It's like everybody in the room was studying each other. One thing about this nigga, he stood down from no one.

Soon as Dior saw Kole, standing in the living room, she

charged at him, throwing punches. He, just like everyone in the room, felt her hurt because he stood there allowing her to hit him until she was tried.

"I deserved that!"

"Is my baby alive?"

"That's why I'm here, D. You got something that belongs to me."

"The fuck I got for you?" Watching them was like watching a Lifetime movie. Jare felt some type of way, though, and I wanted to laugh so bad.

"That's two million dollars you took."

"You here for money, really?"

"Look, you get my money back to me, then you can have Chyna back and also, kill that bitch Karma. I never wanted to hurt you this way, but at the time, I was offered a nice deal. If it would've worked out, I would have come back for you."

35

Dior

I jerked my hands away from Kole as he grabbed it, I couldn't believe what he was saying. He took my child to raise with another bitch because she promised him a set life. Then on top of that he was trying to sell her back to me.

"Look, I know this is a lot of you right now. Just think about it and give me a call," he said as he handed me a card with his number on it. I watched as he walked out the door before I spoke.

Turning to Paris and speaking directly to her, I got in her face and looked her straight in her eyes. "Bring my baby back like you promised!" I placed the card in her hand and walked away from where she was. I never in a billion years thought Kole would turn out to be this type of person.

I just laid in my bed and balled up in a knot crying my eyes out. It had been five years since I took that money, and I had never touched it. I didn't know why, but it was like I had a feeling I would someday need it again. Money was nothing to me, so I would give Kole exactly what he wanted. Lord, this world we lived in was cruel. But placing Paris and her family in my life was a blessing.

Looking at Paris, you wouldn't know she was as thorough as she was. She was so preserved and laid back, she walked and talked like she had money. But she never spoke her personal life. Seeing her handle, me the way she did earlier kind of put me in my feelings. She sat in the chair she was in like she was a boss, and I admired her and prayed to someday have the strength that she had.

"You good?"

Jare walked in the room, looking like a Hersey's kiss. His dark chocolate skin was smooth like mocha, he kept a fresh fade, and his beard was trimmed by one of God's angels. He smelled like Bond No. 9 cologne and when he licked his lips the seat of my panties would always get wet. I looked at him and stared at the many tattoos that were on his arms and neck before I spoke.

"Yeah, just got a lot on my mind!"

"Don't let Paris upset you the way she did earlier. She's just trying to protect you; she has seen enough to survive out here."

"What you trying to say about me, Jare? I have taken care of myself before I knew how to wipe my pussy. I taught myself to wipe from front to back, I had no mother or father. I know how to survive, and until you walk in on both of your parents overdosed, don't tell me anything about surviving." I looked up at him with a mug this time. I wasn't crying, I was pissed. There was no way he was going to sit up here and tell me Paris knew more about surviving then I did. Look at this damn house she had come up in; she knew nothing about struggle.

Surviving was taught to her; the shit came natural to

me. Had her dad not been in the streets as deep as he was it wouldn't have been taught to her. He was just preparing her to live without him. Jare knew nothing about me and for him to say that had pissed me off.

"Look, I ain't tryna piss you off, all I'm saying is she has been through enough to not act off emotions. The way you went in that house earlier could have gotten us all killed. Just think about if your daughter would have been in that house when you went in there."

"Dior, I got you, bruh, we all do honestly. I promise we will do everything to bring baby girl back." I hugged Jare because in my heart I believed him. Since the day he met me, he reassured me that he had my back. I pulled back from him and just starred in his eyes before kissing him.

His mouth tasted just like Hennessy and gum as our tongues joined together, dancing around. He lifted my shirt over my head and began to take my breast in one by one. Laying me back on the bed, and placing a condom on his hard dick, he slid it in me.

"I promise I got you, bruh!" I had never felt so secure before in my life. I began to moan out in pleasure as he flipped me over and drilled in me, pulling my hair. I needed to be thinking about getting my daughter back, but Jare had a bitch nutting back to back and shaking like a fucking leaf.

As bad as I wanted to tap out, I chose against it. My pussy wanted this man as she began to squirt everywhere, the wetness of my pussy ran down my legs. With hi' plugging in and out of me, and the gripped around my hair getting tighter, what I said next was a simple relax of good dick.

"I love you!"

"I love you too... now get up and come ride daddy

dick." Just like that, I got on top of him with my back facing him. I reached down, grabbed his ankles, and I gave him the ride of his life. I don't know if I really loved him or that's how good the dick was hitting. But after fucking all night, we laid in each other arms and being there felt so right.

Before drifting off to sleep, I said a silent prayer asking God for strength, patience, and forgiveness for whatever I was about to go do. I wouldn't be able to just chill and allow somebody else to go get my child and bring her back to me. It was bad enough she would know who I am, I had to be the one to get her.

THE NEXT DAY, I woke up feeling like I could conquer the world. I guess that's what good dick will do to you. Jare wasn't in the bed when I woke up and that was fine because I needed to get some shit handled today. I showered and handled my hygiene and threw on a PINK outfit by Victoria Secret.

Walking downstairs, Meech, Jare, and Paris were all sitting around the table, talking. But once I got close, they stopped, I rolled my eyes and just kept walking out the door. I was pissed the fuck off, and I felt as if they were hiding something for some unknown reason. If I was being a burden on them, they would need to let me know.

"Dior!"

"Yeah"." I turned to see Paris walk up behind me. At this point, I was real fucking aggravated, but couldn't help but notice how her scared surgery had her looking like her old self. She was pretty as fuck, and her looks wouldn't have you thinking she wasn't as gutta as she was.

She was wearing a pair of all-white Air Max with a Nike outfit. I learned she loved her tennis as well as keeping herself up with the latest things. I couldn't be mad at Paris because she was only out here to help me.

"Look, I ain't about to let you go out there and handle this shit alone."

"What makes you think I'm going to fuck with that?"

"Girl, I ain't crazy. I saw the way you studied Kole's number last night. I bet you got it memorized, if you don't want them to know then cool. But I'm going with you."

As she said that, she walked around the passenger side of me Tiffany blue Camaro and got in. I needed to do this myself, but I knew going alone would be crazy. Instead of fussing with her, I got in the car and pulled off.

"I need to go to the bank and get this money."

"So, you did take his money?"

"I ain't take shit, and I didn't know he was faking his death. I would've been a damn fool to leave that much money there. If they needed it that bad, he would've told his side bitch to take the money","" I said, feeling myself get angry all over.

I turned up the music and allowed Kevin Gates to blast through the speakers. I grabbed a pre-rolled blunt from the middle console and fired it up. Passing it to Paris, I let the smoke fill my lungs and felt a release come over my body.

This was about to be a long day, but Kole and his bitch had played with the wrong bitch. Fucking with my daughter and hiding from me all these years was the worse thing ever. I wasn't about to sit around and wait for them to come up with a plan. I was going to kill these bitches with my bare hands if I had to.

"You got the money?"

"Yep!" I pulled out my phone and placed a text to Kole.

ME: Got the money!

A few minutes later, he hit me back with an address, and Paris and I waited around until it was time to go meet him. I knew I should be placing a call to Jare, but after it was all said and done, he would be proud of me for bossing up without him.

36

Paris

I was riding with Dior, but I was no fucking fool, so I had
already placed a text to Meech and Jare, telling them to
meet us uptown. I understood Dior was going to get her
daughter back no matter what it took, but going in this
alone was a suicide mission. There was no way, I was about
to trust Kole or his bitch. Why the fuck would you come
alone to meet a nigga that faked his death and raised your
child with a fake ass nanny bitch?

Laying back in my seat, allowing the smoke to pene-
trate my lungs, I watched as Dior bit down on her nails. I
just shook my head and grabbed my phone from my
pocket.

'*The fuck*,' I thought as I opened my Instagram app and
saw a picture of Cassidy and Gus together. He hadn't
posted a picture in so long; I didn't even know I still
followed him. I clicked on his page and looked at all of the
pictures of them and their son. My palms started to fill
with sweat as I took a screenshot and sent it to Meech.

The one picture that took me overboard was the one
with Koti, sitting beside Cassidy and it was as if they were

living a stress-free life. I couldn't believe they were on social media, posting pictures as if they didn't make my life a living hell.

"That's him right there!" I looked up from my phone toward the black-on-black Challenger Dior pointed toward as we watched Kole get out. We had been sitting so long that it was now dark outside.

"He don't have my baby with him, though." I nodded and sent a text to Meech as we got ready to get out the car.

"You good, Dior?"

"Just ready to get all of this over with."

Soon as we reached Kole, Dior threw the bags at his feet, but before he could grab them, I reached for them, jerking them up from the ground. She was never to make a swap without getting her daughter.

"The fuck you doing, Paris?"

"You don't know if he has your daughter for sure." I looked at her sideways, then turned my attention back to him. "Where's her daughter?"

"She's with Karma; I couldn't take her with me, she wouldn't allow me to take her with me." I looked from Dior to Kole and rolled my eyes. Had she come on her own, she would have been jacked.

PEW!

PEW!

PEW!

The sound of gunshots caused me to jump for cover, grabbing Dior, and pulling her down with me.

"NO! He's taking the money without giving me my baby."

She jumped from the ground and started to run behind Kole, but my body was burning so bad. I just laid there, grabbing the spot where my stomach cramped. I pulled my hand to my face and saw so much blood.

"Paris! Paris!"

I hated myself for coming out here with Dior, instead of waiting on Meech and Jare. However, I knew letting her go alone would be much worse than what I was. Kole was really playing with fire.

"Shit it hurts!" I felt my body lift from the ground and knew I was in Meech's arms. I laid my head on his shoulders as everything around me went black.

37

Jare

"I fucking told you that I got you." I was so mad; I had wrapped my arms around Dior's neck and was trying to choke the fuck out of her. Feeling Meech grab me to calm down was the only reason I stopped. Other than that, I would have killed this bitch. I had to walk out the hospital before I punched the hoe down right where she stood.

My sister was in the back fighting for her life because Dior's dumb ass wanted to go to war without some real goons. I watched the whole exchanged, and had Paris not been there shit would have been worse. Then she had the nerve to leave my sister on the ground and run behind Kole. I was tired of fucking with these Dizzy Dora ass hoes.

"She just wanted her child, Jare"," Queen said as she walked up behind me and rubbed my back. She had become my mother since finding out King was my father. It was nothing I wouldn't do for her and vice versa.

"She should have just waited until it was the right time for all of us to go. Paris is back there fighting for her damn life because of her dumb ass decisions."

"Son, behind your child you will do whatever, whenever, and not give not one fuck who is doing. We can't blame Dior for going out there, it was Paris's choice to go with her. Your dad has been in the game for years, and the same thing has happened to me. I felt he was moving too slow to get a lot of shit handled, so I handled it alone and ended up in far worse situations. That girl has been without her child for five years, thinking she was dead, I don't blame her for not wanting to waste another second away."

"Ugh!" I punched the brick wall that stood behind me, immediately drawing blood from my knuckles. I was fucking irritated at this dumb ass moves this bitch had made. Queen explained that shit great, but, still in all, my sister was shot in the process, and she let Kole stupid ass jack her.

"Let's go in here and get your hand checked on."

Walking back in the hospital, holding my hand Dior rain up to me, grabbing it. I pushed her back and walked over to the nurses' station, seeking help. My hand was beginning to swell.

"Jare, just talk to me please!"

"Bitch, I don't wanna talk to you, I don't even want you around me right now"," I said through gritted teeth.

"You're acting real fucking childish right now, Jare. You mad because I went after my daughter. Really?"

"No, dumb ass I'm mad because you tried to go behind my back when I told you over and over again, I had you. My sister in the back fighting for her life and you could have possibly been hurt too." She grabbed my arm again and before I knew it, I reached out and pushed her, causing her to fall over.

I no longer even needed my arm checked out, I was just that fucking mad. I would call my homegirl who was a nurse to come by later, and check me out. I'm sure it wasn't broken 'cause I could still move it around.

"Call me later, Ma!" I said to Queen before walking out the hospital doors. As bad as I wanted to stay and make sure that Paris was straight, but had Dior not been so dumb, we wouldn't be here.

"You lashing out on her for nothing, lil' brudda!"

"Meech, you my nigga, but stay out this. I got every right to lash out on the bitch for doing that dumb ass shit." He threw his hands up and backed away from where we stood.

"I don't want no smoke, Big General!" I got in my car and peeled off, leaving Meech standing on the curb. They couldn't tell me how to feel, I had started to love Dior. I wasn't mad that she tried to save her child, but more so that she could have gotten herself killed.

She wasn't thinking and was being selfish as fuck when she pulled that move. I didn't want to lose her, and I was just getting to know her. She was far from Cassidy and everything about her, even her natural body odor, was pure. After thinking about how I acted, I knew I needed to do something to make up.

"Woah, what's up?" I spoke into the phone talking to my nigga Conrad. He was one of my homies from around the way, but he was one of them nerdy niggas. He stayed in the hood, but whenever I called him, he already knew what the deal was.

"I can't call it, brudda... what we got today?"

"I need you to track down Kole Lemar, and send me an address on that nigga, ASAP."

"Bet; hit you back in ten."

I laid back in my seat and decided to wait until he hit me back. Five minutes later, he had hit me back with an address and pictures on this fool. I don't know how the fuck he had done it, and I wasn't about to ask no questions. I placed a call to Meech and went to the crib to get suited up. I was killing Kole and his bitch today. There was no doubt in my mind that I wasn't going to bring baby girl back home with me.

38

Meech

Most muthafuckas would get the fuck out of dodge when they pulled something so stupid off. Paris hadn't come out of surgery yet, but I had to go handle Kole's ass before he came to his senses and leave. I couldn't allow another muthafucka to touch something that was mine, then get away with it.

"I need to go handle something," I said to King. I'm sure he already knew what I was up to. He gave me a knowing look, and told me he would keep me updated.

I hated the way Jare handled the situation with Dior, but I understood he was mad. But Paris was grown as fuck even though she was texting us her every move. I still was feeling some type of way that she got in the car with Dior, instead of just stopping her, and waiting on us. I couldn't get to her fast enough when I saw those bullets pierce through her body.

Honestly, I never thought things would go down the way they had gone down. Kole had been playing a dangerous fucking game, then had the nerve to be laid up in a hotel. He would get exactly what the fuck was coming to him tonight.

"My lil' potna work in here, and he's going to cut the cameras, and I already paid the chick at the front desk for a key. It's been confirmed they have a child in there with them"," Jare spoke while taking a pull from the blunt, and loading up his guns.

We got out the car and walked through the back door where Jare's potna stood holding it open. I grabbed both guns from my waist and began to cock them back. Catching the employee elevator, we reached the fifth floor and walked to room 510 where Kole and his girl were staying. Some chick Jare knew was standing outside the room to grab Chyna.

Gaining access to go in the room, I stood over the bed where Kole and Karma peacefully slept while baby girl was in the bed by herself. I grabbed her up, and reached her to the girl in the hallway, and watched as they disappeared.

"Wake up!" I kicked the bed and brought my gun down in Kole's stomach.

"Urgh!"

"Yeah, buddy get the fuck up you can't sleep while my lil' sister fighting for her life."

"Where the fuck is my daughter?"

"You mean Dior's daughter?" I spoke, looking at Karma sideways. I don't think I have even run across a bitch this crazy, this was some Lifetimes shit.

"Kole, you made a deal with my girl, but you didn't pull through with it."

"Man, look, whatever you want you can have just don't kill us."

I had to laugh at how he was begging for his life while his bitch sat on side of him not even mumbling a word.

She was more gangsta than her pussy ass boyfriend. This shit was funny as fuck, but I needed to get back to the hospital. Standing back, both me and Jare lift our guns up and lit bodies up. It was like a damn Scarface movie the way the lead entered their bodies, and they began to jerk from the impact.

POW!

POW!

I quickly put a bullet between both of there eyes, grabbed the bags full of money, and left out as quick as I came in. Reaching the night air, I grabbed Dior's daughter and made my way back to the hospital. Jare had grabbed both of us a change of clothes. What happened tonight no one would speak on again. For the way Kole had done my girl, I had no other choice but to take him out.

"Where's are we going?" I looked back at how beautiful Dior's daughter was and knew this would brighten up her day. At least something good will come out of all the bad that had been happening in life.

"To see your mommy!" The car grew silent, and I turned the music up, resting my head on the seat that I sat in. These people were going to be the fucking death of me.

"HOW IS SHE?" I asked as I walked into the lobby where everyone was still seated.

"She just got out of surgery, and they were able to remove all three bullets and get her sedated. She's going to make a speedy recovery, Meech." I watched as Queen smiled, and I knew she felt the same way I did. It was like she, nor Paris, would ever be able to catch a break, but we would soon live peacefully. I could bet my life on that.

"Chyna!" Dior screamed as she ran to where her

daughter and Jare stood. There was excitement on her face and Queen cried even more than she was before. I knew it would take some time for baby girl to come around, but she had to know that she as now home.

39

Dior

Everything had been going good since the day Jare walked into the hospital with Chyna. It took her some time to adjust, but she as happy like hell she wasn't going back to Karma. After hearing how mean she was to her, I wish I could find her and break the bitch's neck.

We all decided to move out of King and Queen's crib and get our own. Meech and Paris got them a nice mini-mansion that sat by the water. My girl was truly a soldier; she had been through a lot and was able to overcome it all. She walked with a limp, but it wouldn't be long before she was back to her old self.

After the things I had gone through in life, I prayed for peace and within this family, I had gotten that. I was so lost in this world on my own until I met Paris, she and her family treated me like one of their own since the first time they had met me.

"I love the view of your house." Paris and I sat on the balcony and watched as Price and Chyna played the back-yard. The guys were gone as usual, but it no longer bothered me, I had gotten use to Jare running the streets, then coming in with gifts later that night. I expected them, but I still wanted my man in the bed with me.

"Yeah, I love it here! Queen calls me every day trying to convince me to move back there. We lived on two different sides, and she barely saw me. But I know she's getting lonely with all of us gone."

"Queen is a mess, she called me earlier asking what I was doing for Jare's birthday. So much had been going on, I forgot his shit was coming up."

"Damn, me too! I'ma tell King we throwing a party at Allure this weekend. My dawg has been through a lot, he deserves a quick turn up."

"Shid, put that in the works, and I'll see about getting him a nice gift. He has been my rib since the day I met him." We laughed at how I was starting to adapt to Baton Rouge. I often found myself talking country just like them. 'I couldn't formulate a sentence without cursing, but I was beginning to love it here.

"Hey, bae!" Later that night, I was lying in bed, reading a book by Authoress Lem when Jare walked in the room and kissed me on my forehead. Even after being out all day he still seemed to always smell so good. I thought I knew love when I was with Kole, but the love with Jare was different. He had become everything I dreamed of and more.

"How was your day?" I looked over at Jare as he sat in the chair, in the corner of the room, and he was knocked out. I took his clothes off and threw a cover on him. Since getting Chyna back, he had been in the streets like crazy. We had more than enough money for him to retire, but he was so deep in.

He could rest now, though, 'cause come this weekend, we were going to turn Allure the fuck up. I was going to make sure my man had the time of his life as we took over the club for one night. Earlier, I put everything into play when I was with Paris and tomorrow, I would be picking up his 2019 Wraith. Jare deserved everything for the way he had been treating me and my baby. Never had I been treated like a queen before, but he made sure that all our needs were met.

Tori: Hope you made it in safe!

I looked over at Jare's phone as it vibrated from the nightstand. As bad as I wanted to jump to conclusion, I knew that wasn't the way things worked. I had dealt with cheating before and if my mother hadn't taught me anything, she taught me to believe none of what I hear and half of what I see. I got in the bed and just went to sleep, but I'm sure those texts would be on my mind. But I would give him the chance to tell me who Tori was.

━━━

ALLURE WAS PACKED as the line wrapped around the building. Paris was already in the section, throwing back shots and dancing. The vibe was a laid back one, and I was giving Jare a lap dance and enjoying being in the company of my man.

"'What's up, Jay?" I looked up at the woman that stood before us and immediately wiped the smile off my face. She resembled that Instagram model Ari, she had the body and all. I had to give it to her, besides me and my bestie, she was one of the baddest women in this club.

"What's good, Tori?

'*Tori*,' I thought to myself as I looked her up and down, then directed my attention back to my nigga. I would not cause a scene tonight, I would remain calm. I had honestly forgot about her texting the phone the other night and moved passed it. But I was standing in the middle of them as they were giving each other sweet eyes and Jare had yet to introduce me.

"What's good, Big Meech?" Meech looked at Paris before he spoke back. I was pissed, but I couldn't help but laugh at how scared Paris had him to speak to another woman. Since the last incident that nigga ain't give another bitch enough time to even she was in the same room as him.

"Hi, my name is Dior since my man is being so rude."

"Damn, Jay, you ain't tell me you had a girl last night."

Yep she wanted to get her face slapped. Paris stayed seated on this couch; verbally she would never open her mouth when it involved me and Jare getting into something. But I knew she wouldn't let a fight between me, and this bitch go down. Actually, I didn't need her to jump in my hands worked real well.

I had paid too much to enjoy this party, though, so I wouldn't be caught dead fighting in these 1,500-dollar red bottoms. My dress cost more than this hoe's entire existence. Walking away from where I was standing, I went to take a seat by Paris, and just bobbed my head to the music.

I couldn't even trip I had planned this whole party for him, got him a new car, and he was in here with another female. It was rough coming up in Miami, so I promised myself when I made it out, I wouldn't live the same life. I promised myself that I would change, but sitting here, I wanted nothing more than to get up and show my fucking ass in this club.

"You good, stank?" Paris asked, screaming over the loud music.

"Girl, yes!"

Shid, I was beyond good, and I wasn't about to sweat a damn thing about Jare like she sidy. At least, I wouldn't sweat him in public the shit ain't worth it, he can have this show. He was so caught up in ole girl that he allowed her to disrespect me.

"I'm about to get up out here!"

"Seriously?" Paris turned to look at me with an aggravated expression on her face. "You put all of this together and you leaving because of her. As long as you walk this Earth don't ever make a bitch feel she got that much power over you."

"Dude not even talking to me right now!"

"And! You don't even know the relationship between the two. Act like a lady in public, and a donkey when y'all make it home. Chill out and relax; if she gets out of hand, we on that hoe head." A bitch on the streets would swear Paris was boujee until she opened her mouth and spoke. She was a nigga in a female's body and she often posed a threat to bitches and niggas.

"Bet!"

40

Paris

I was sitting back, watching the whole play between Jare and the bitch that stood before him. I hated for Cassidy to get in me and Meech's shit, so I knew not to jump in their business. However, I was going to talk to Jare whenever we made it home. Because he was being disrespectful to his girl.

"Who ole girl is?" I asked Meech.

"Her and Jare go all the way back, she grew up in Haynes with us." I nodded my head as he spoke without taking my attention off the two of them. Dior was sitting on the side of me, in her feelings, but she needed to get the fuck out them. Tori was, bad but my bitch was badder, and she was not about to sit up here and let nobody play on her top. If she wanted attention, or a reaction, she would play the same game he's playing.

She went all out for this nigga's birthday and he was in here acting as if she's wasn't even five feet away from him. He was my brother, but I was a woman before I was anything, and I know how it felt to be publicly hurt.

"Snatch a nigga up, and enjoy your night," I leaned

over and whispered in Dior's ear. She was hesitant to do it, but she got up and went to the dance floor. I stood to my feet and walked over where Jare was and looked over the balcony. Dior was dancing to "Hot Girl Summer" by Meg with a nigga.

I felt a strong wind fly pass me and smirked, I continued to watch as Jare went and punched the dude down and yanked Dior out the club. She wanted her nigga's attention well, now she got it, and he couldn't be mad at her when he stood in her face with another bitch all night. I turned to mug Tori, then left the section with Meech, following behind me.

"Ya girl Tori is going to be trouble," I said to Meech as soon as we stepped foot outside.

"I doubt it; she's not that type of girl at all, and let me find out you pushed Dior up to something that stupid."

"Hey, Meech." Tori ran up and caught up to us.

"Tell Jare to come by the house later, and see me if he can get away."

"Girl, fuck no, he ain't telling Jare shit. If you want to talk to my brother, I suggest you do so it in front of his girl."

"Since when did Jare get a sister."

"The day our dad dropped me from his nut sack."

"Come on, P! Tori's cool people, man, chill out."

I looked at Meech and walked away, he knew better than to defend a bitch in my presence. Something wasn't right with her and Jare, I wouldn't speak on it, but I was no fool.

Making it home, I walked in the house full speed and slammed the door behind me. I was pissed at Meech for basically correcting me in front of Tori, and I was starting to think they both were fucking her. As a man, he should have stopped Jare, and I can only imagine what they do in public.

"The fuck you around here slamming doors for?"

"Y'all niggas straight bullshit!"

"So, you pissed at me because Jare invited an old friend? Yeah, you women are crazier than I thought. I just find it funny how you kept telling Cassidy to mind her business, but you doing the same shit she did."

"Don't compare us 'cause I'm nothing like the bitch. I'm pissed because Dior went all out for his birthday and he had the damn nerve to ignore her the whole night. I had to literally beg her to stay at a fucking party she threw."

"Paris, I understand you frustrated, but I'm not about to fuss with you about somebody else's business. I'm high and tipsy, and I wanted to come home and get in that pussy, not fuss about people that don't even live in the same home as us."

I had to have been bipolar because the mention of him getting in my guts made me smile and drop all my clothes right where I stood. Meech picked me up and carried me up the stairs to our bedroom. Laying me across the bed, he took his hat off and began to devour my pussy. My juices instantly started flooding and splashing everywhere.

My fiancé knew exactly what points to hit to make me ready to run up a wall. After he made me squirt with his mouth, I pushed him down on the bed and took all ten inches of his dick into my mouth, and began to hum as I bobbed my head up and down. Spitting on the tip, I took both hands and began to beat the dick as I sucked it harder and harder. Whoever said you 'can't make a man nut with head was a lie because I licked and sucked up each drop of nut that poured from his dick until he was empty.

I looked him in his eyes and sucked him back up,

making his dick rock hard. Climbing on top, I placed both feet on the bed and bounced up and down on his shaft. I was no Meg thee Stallion, but I was working the fuck out this nigga and his moans let me know, I was doing a damn good job.

"Damn, P! It feels so good, bruh." I slowed my pace down and placed my hands on the headboard as I leaned down and began to passionately kiss him. This ride had been rocky for the both of us, but we had overcome so much.

"Let's get married now!"

"No, I want a big wedding," as I said that, Meech rolled me over and began to pound in and out of me from the back. He wrapped my ponytail around his hands and went harder and harder until I creamed all over his dick.

"Shit, bae, slow down!"

"I'm about to nut"…" He grunted as we collapsed and laid in the same spot for what seemed like forever.

"I want to get married next weekend, find a venue, and there's no price limit." I looked at Meech with my head cocked to the side. This man had just dicked me down, then demand we get married in a week. I knew my pussy was good, but shit, I ain't think I was packing that much power.

I wanted to marry him too, but I wanted everything to be perfect. I didn't want to feel as if we were rushing things and everything fell apart. Getting up from the bed, I walked into the bathroom and took a shower. It was already after three in the morning and Meech had worn me out. If I wanted to have a successful wedding, I needed to rest my mind, body, and soul.

41

Jare

Man, I ain't have a thing to say to Dior since she wanted to be out here acting like a thot. I ain't say shit to her since I punched that nigga in his shit and grabbed her up out the club. The way she was in there acting was uncalled for. Her spot in my life was solidified and catching up with an old friend should not be a threat to her.

I decided to drop her off home and make some moves through the city. Being in the house with her right now would not be good. She really had me thinking, though. I understood she was mad, but did she hoe around every time shit ain't go her way? She could stay by herself and think things through.

First, I was going to go stay by my pops house, but I didn't want to hear Queen lecturing me on making things work. Whenever I was pissed off, I needed to be alone in order to get my temper under control.

ME: Drop ya location!

I shot Tori a text and waited until she sent her location, I knew this wouldn't be a good idea. However, I missed her, and seeing her the other day was the greatest gift. Tori wasn't like any other girl back in the days, she was my Bonnie. She was a rider and you wouldn't see me without her.

The day she left had to be the worse day of my life and after her, it was hard for me to trust again. She took my heart when her parents decided to up and move because of a job her father had gotten out of town. The only woman that made that better was Dior, but the way she carried on tonight had me thinking maybe she was like Cassidy.

"What's up?" I said as I walked in Tori's crib. I had to give it to her, she had a nice little layout in her crib, I nodded in approval.

"Your girl did the most back at the club, huh?"

"Yeah, she don't normally act that way."

I hadn't come here to talk about Dior because the thought of how she had disrespected me at the club just kept playing over and over in my head. But I knew being here was a bad idea. Tori stood in front me with a robe on and nothing under it. Her body was still perfect just as it was when we were eighteen.

"Why you looking at me like that?"

"You still as beautiful as the day we first met."

Tori seductively walked over to me and dropped her robe down to her ankles. I had no business doing this, I should've gone to my pops crib. But I much rather be here and that was just the God honest truth.

"I missed you, Jay!"

"i missed you too!"

Knock!

Knock!

"You expecting somebody?"

"No, but hold tight while I go get the door." She placed her robe back on and walked away to the door. This was nothing but God because I knew it wouldn't be a good idea. Despite the shit Dior and I had been through, in such a short time, I loved her so much.

POW!

I jumped at the sound of a gun going off and ran toward to the door. Looking at Tori's body on the ground, and Dior standing over her did something to me as a man. I saw the hurt in her eyes, and I knew then I had fucked up

"I knew it was more than just a friendship between the two of you. Her death is on your hands, and I want you out the fucking house." I looked down at Tori as she laid on the floor with her eyes open.

"D, let me explain!" She walked away without saying so much of a word. It was literally after five in the morning, and I was out here dealing with this shit. I would talk to Dior once I got home. Grabbing the phone, I called the only person, I knew would come through without judging me.

Forty minutes later, Paris was pulling up with a mug on her face. She was pissed when I told her where I was. But I knew she would come through.

"Let's hurry before Meech realizes I'm gone," she said as she threw all the things to me that I asked her to bring. I knew she was mad, but now was not the time to talk about anything.

Tori stayed in a nice neighborhood, so if we were to get caught, we would literally be facing life in prison. So, burning the house down would be our best out. There would be no clues left behind. I grabbed the can of gas from the floor and poured it everywhere. Lighting a match, I threw it on the floor, then got the fuck out of dodge.

Both me and Paris went our separate ways without saying another word to one another. I knew without a doubt my sister would always have my back, but this time around she was pissed the fuck off. I had to go check with my girl, though, and make sure she was straight, I hated that she had to catch me at Tori's house.

'While all the time that I was loving you, you was busy loving
yourself
I would stop breathing if you told me to, now you busy loving someone
else—'

Soon as I walked in and heard her playing Mary, I turned my duck ass around and went by my pops crib. I knew she was hurting entirely too bad for us to have a decent conversation tonight.

"Was it worth it?" Queen walked in the kitchen where I was sitting and rubbed my back.

"I didn't want to come here for this very reason alone."

"Why? You didn't want me to tell you that you were wrong?"

"I'll tell Dior to stop calling you whenever we have a problem."

"She didn't call me; you woke me when the alarm went off. I don't know what the problem is with the two of you, but considering it the break of dawn and you're down here drinking. I know it must have been something bad." She sighed before talking again.

"Look, I know, I'm not your mother and I'm not trying to fill her spot. However, being that you are my husband's son and my stepchild, I have to be real with you. Mutha-fuckas in the streets are going to be disloyal to you or feel it's easy to aim for you if you aren't showing loyalty to what's at home. Don't be so caught up in what's going on and miss what's standing right before you. I ain't the best person to take advice from because I have fucked up time after time, and your father has as well. But together we are strong, and muthafuckas go through hell to tear us down.

Apart we are both weak and lose concentration of that game that's before us. Notice how you and Meech had to step up when we were separated, we feed off each other's energy. Any other time, I would have said go up and get some rest, but not this time. I have Prince and Chyna in the guest room asleep, so you need to go home and work your relationship out. Don't be so thirsty behind these half-naked females that throw themselves at you. They are just waiting for a moment to destroy what you have at home, because they want it."

As bad as I wanted to go upstairs and get some sleep before talking to Dior, it could wait. I needed to fix shit between us because everything Queen had spoken was the truth. A part of it was easy for muthafuckas to attack what we had worked so hard to accomplish. Out of all the shit, I had seen in my years of living, seeing the hurt in Dior's eyes made my heart ache the worse. She didn't deserve to deal with my bullshit. Just like I didn't deserve to have her as my woman, she was too good.

42

Dior

I had a feeling Jare would link up with Tori, so I wasn't about to go in the house when he dropped me off. He pulled off so quickly that he didn't even see me get straight in the car and start to follow behind him. He rode around for the few, then made his way over to her house. The only reason, I got out the car is because he took too long to come out the house.

God is my witness, I never wanted to kill her, but when she saw me on the other side of the door. She had the nerve to have a grin on her face. That had done something to me as a woman. Be she was sitting here, smirking, without any clothes on under her robe. She was flaunting in my face the fact that she had my man then, and was about to have him now.

I couldn't seem weak, so I told him to get the fuck out whenever he finished cleaning the bitch up. I wasn't about to be that bitch that sat around and allowed her man to cheat whenever he got ready. Over the past few years, I had been through entirely too much and was starting to think maybe relationships weren't for me. Maybe I needed to just be alone and deal with myself.

"Dior, let's talk!" I was knocked out sleep when Jare came in, shaking me. I sat up in the bed, and wiped my eyes. Honestly, I was over the apology stages. The more a man apologized, the less I loved him. I didn't want that to be me and Jare, but I was nearing my point and it hadn't been long for us.

"I know you pissed at me, but I didn't do anything with Tori. No lie, I was about to, but you came and killed her, she was a blast from the past. She was my first love, and seeing her had brought back some memories for me. Nothing more, nothing less." I looked at Jare's narrowed eyes and turned the lamp off that was on the nightstand beside the bed. Shid, she was now a distant memory, so I wasn't about to trip.

"Get in the bed!" I said before dozing back off to sleep.

As mad as I was, I just wasn't about to fight behind somebody that was dead. The next time, he gets caught, if there is a next time, he would be going with her. I had been getting fucked over since I was a child, and I refuse to keep allowing people to do the same fucking thing to me. Being out there in the jungle with wolves gave you a different mindset. I was cut from a different cloth, and I would kill a bitch before I allowed any disrespect.

43

Paris

"Then the crazy bitch told me to get in the bed with her."

"Yeah, put that over there and call Meech to go get fitted for his tux."

Jare had been here running down to me what happened between him and Dior while I was at the venue, getting straight for the wedding. Dior had me cracking up, she had already called me and gave me the rundown. Had my poor brother so nervous he was asking can he spend the night at my house.

"Paris, what I do?"

"For starters, you got a good female at home, and you out here in the streets wilding out. You had no business leaving your girl at home after she had just balled out for your birthday to be with ya ex-bitch. You stood in the club and disrespected her, then you allowed Tori to do the same. I ain't taking no sides because you know how I feel about that shit. But, at the end of the day, I'm a woman and the way you went about shit at the club would make any bitch act up."

"I understand I was wrong, but she ain't have to go

dance on another nigga. That shit was embarrassing and fucking disrespectful." I looked at Jare and cocked my head to the side. I couldn't believe he was standing here contradicting himself.

"The wedding is two days away have that shit figured out by then. I don't need nobody ruining my day with fucked-up attitudes."

"Gotcha, Big Gangsta; you a bridezilla out this fucking world." We both laughed, and continued making sure things were in order. My big day was slowly approaching, and I wanted everything to be perfect. The closer it got, the more nervous I was. But I had waited my whole damn life for this shit, and I wasn't about to allow anyone to ruin it.

On the drive home, I turned the radio down and decided to have a talk with God. A few years ago, I asked him for peace and hadn't talked to him since. I would thank him throughout the day, but I needed him to know how much I appreciated him.

God, I come to you humbly and calm. It may have been some time since I've had a full out conversation with you, but I need you to know how thankful I am for you. A while back, I was lost and thinking the world was against me. I never thought I'll get a second chance at love until you sent Prince my way. I never thought Meech and I would be here, or that I would have a bond so tight with a sibling. You sent me Dior when I was in a weak spot and she helped me trust females again. God, I thank you because you turned around all the bad in my life, and for that alone I am grateful. Seeing my parents back together and everyone around me in peace it makes me feel as though things won't change again.

In Jesus name, Amen!

44

Cassidy

Hearing that Meech and Paris were getting married from my grandmother angered me more than I was already angry. Come to find out, I had contracted AIDS from this corner boy I was dealing with. Gus got tested and he as well came back negative. But once I told Peddie, he confirmed that he knew he had it, but didn't think I'll get it by fucking one time. I killed that bitch right where he stood.

There were days, I was angry at myself, but I decided to just take my medicine and some classes, so that I could live a healthy life. I was still raising my son, so I didn't want him growing up without me. After the shit with Karma fell through, we were all on our ass and low on money.

One day, I ran into Karma coming out of the pharmacy; she and I knew each other from going to elementary school together. She moved around so much, so she didn't stay long. After chilling and catching up, she told me about Dior, and just like that I put her up on game. We were all supposed to split the money, but when I saw Jare and

Meech walk out their hotel, I knew I wouldn't be getting shit.

I promised Meech that I would be good and stay out the way in exchange for me living. My grandmother only had the two of us, and I knew it would kill her if I didn't go to his wedding. I had no intentions on getting out the way with them, I was going to be by my grandmother's side.

Gus felt it was a bad idea while Koti, on the other hand, wanted to crash the wedding and cause more drama. We were able to live this long with them gunning for us. Without Meech, she didn't want to live, but I was going to stay out the fucking way. I hated all them for the way, they had done me too, but I knew not to cross them.

"I'm going to that wedding and getting my daughter."

"You don't think that maybe she's in a better place? We live from motel to motel barely even have food, and you want to bring her here."

"You have your son!"

"But I have no other choice both his parents are here. Meech is taking good care of Riley, I don't suggest you go there fucking with them, Koti. You know Meech as well as I do, and you know he ain't about to let you walk out the venue if you walk in there."

"And he's going to let you go free?"

"I honestly don't know, and I don't care, at the moment. I'm going because my grandmother invited me, and I was once a part of that family."

Going to this wedding would never be a great idea, but I had to see my cousin get married. I refused to not be there, and we were so close growing up. As much as I hated Paris, I knew they were meant to be together. I still couldn't believe she hooked Jare up with Dior after he and

I broke up. She was supposed to remain loyal to me, no matter what I had gone through.

The venue where they were getting married was downtown and it was beautiful. I grabbed my grandmother's hand and walked in to be seated. My hair was in a curly bush, and I wore some dark shades, so no one would recognize me. I wasn't on any drama and didn't want them looking at me crazy.

Just as we were seated, the groomsmen and Meech walked from the back and went to stand by the preacher. My cousin looked so handsome in all white as his dreads hung and were in twist. I dabbed the tears that flowed down my cheeks when I looked up Jare was staring directly at me with a mug. He leaned over to whisper something in Meech's ear, then they both brought their attention to me.

I grabbed my grandmother's hand tight as the sweat beads rolled down my face. Meech looked at me the whole time the bridesmaids walked down the aisle, and I was just waiting for someone to yank me up. But he allowed the wedding to go on, and I let out a sigh of relief. Maybe he had a change of heart just like I did; he knew him killing me today would be stupid on his part.

After the wedding, we were all at the reception hall, sitting down waiting to eat. I walked from the table and went to search for a restroom when I was yanked from my feet and brought down to the basement. When I got down there, I locked eyes with Jare, Paris, Meech, and King. I knew this was a bad idea to come here.

"Didn't I tell you if I ever see you again, I would kill you?"

"I've changed since finding out I was sick. Grandma wanted me to come with her, so I told her I would. I swear I'm not here to cause any problems."

"I don't give a fuck about what she asked you to do,

you have fucked over everybody in this family. No one wants you around here, and I told you if you come around again, I would kill you bitch, and I meant that."

"I'll leave Meech!" Just when I said that, Paris came up, slicing the side of my face the same way I had done hers. Gunshots could be heard as I closed my eyes. But I opened them, and I realized I wasn't hit.

"See what the fuck you started now somebody shooting my wedding up."

"They shooting, P, and I don't know what to do blood is everywhere and bodies dropping"," Dior ran in the room and said.

"Kill this bitch and let's go." Meech stood there staring at me, and I knew deep in his heart he didn't want to kill me. No matter what I had done I was still family.

POW!

When the gun went off and a single bullet entered my head. There was a better place than Earth and even though I may not see it. I just wanted everyone to know how truly sorry I was.

45

Koti

Meech stupid if he thought I would allow him to raise my daughter with Paris's spoiled ass. I had been thinking of a plan, but today, was the right fucking day. The whole family was in one room at the same time. I walked with Gus and we both started airing the bitch out. I spotted Queen and put a bullet in her head. I hated the bitch anyways.

I was no killer, but Meech had pushed me to the point of no return. I walked over to where his grandmother laid on the floor and stood over her. He fucked with my family, then I had no other choice but to fuck with his. I didn't care if kids got hit in the process. In a matter of ten minutes, Gus and I had laid just about half of the reception down.

Walking out the hall, I ran straight into Meech's chest. I knew his scent from anywhere, but I don't know why I didn't think to check for him before trying to leave.

"Leaving so soon?" he asked as he grabbed the gun from my hand and pushed me back. With the very same gun, he took and shot Gus repeatedly, then brought it up to me.

"I let you leave peacefully and this how you repay me, Koti"?"

There was screaming from behind us as Paris stood over her mother's body. King ran over to where she stood and brought his hands to his head before breaking down on side of her.

"Bitch!" Paris charged at me so fast, knocking me over punching me repeatedly in my face. I wasn't tripping because I knew what I had done would make them all weak. Queen was the backbone of their family, but without her they would all be in a shit hole.

She stood up and kicked me over and over in the face. I laid there and laughed as I spit blood onto the floor. "Bitch, fighting me won't bring back your mother or your grandmother"," I said to them both.

Meech stood still looking at me with hate when he noticed his grandmother's body on the floor. I had just taken the last thing that meant something to him, and it felt good as fuck. If I did die today, I would die knowing they would suffer from great losses.

Dior walked up to Meech and took the gun out his hand, bringing it to my stomach without thinking twice, she pulled the trigger. She then brought it up to my face and pulled it once more.

46

Paris

ONE YEAR LATER

My past was toxic as fuck, but I managed to escape it. But just when things start looking up, our worlds came tumbling down. Losing Queen and Meech's grandmother was hard on us. The day went down in history as so many lives were taken. I was just grateful Chyna pulled Riley and Prince into a hiding space when she heard the gunshots.

Koti claimed she had come for her daughter, but shot the whole place up, not even caring if her daughter was in the place or not. Meech killed every security he hired, and I couldn't even blame him. Because at that point, I started thinking shit was a fucking setup. I hated to see Cassidy go out the way she did, but she had crossed some lines that were never supposed to be crossed.

It took us a minute to get right after the wedding, but we all pulled through by leaning on one another. King, on the other hand, took the shit hard as fuck and needed more time than we did. I put myself into my boutique and kept my mind off the negative shit around me.

"You ever thought we would be here?" Meech asked as he walked up behind me. After everything went down, we all packed up and moved far, far away. We had our own damn island.

"Yeah, I knew you would take me away from that crazy ass world I was living in." He kissed me, then leaned down and kissed my stomach. I was five months pregnant without baby girl and she was giving me the blues. The closer I felt I was getting, the sicker I was getting.

"I want to thank you, Paris, for making me the man I am. You pushed me and made me realized shit, I never thought I would."

King had officially stepped down and left everything to Jare and Meech. Even though we no longer stayed in the South. The streets were supplied and if you were looking for the white girl, our family was the ones you talked to and everybody knew that. They also knew not to fuck over my family because if one come, they call come.

I wish Queen could see us here today because this is what she wanted. Everybody living and loving each other. Jare had proposed to Dior and they were expected to get married any moment now. Meech put his time into our kids and that's what helped him keep his mind off what happened the night of our wedding.

My father was such a strong and well-kept gentleman. I didn't think anything could ever tear him down, but seeing him split from my mother, then losing her was a different hurt on him. The way Meech catered to me since that day, I can only imagine how he would take it if something was to happen to me.

I grabbed Meech's face and began to kiss him so passionately as he stood there with Versace swim trunks on and the slides to match. I took in his appearance and noticed the tattoo with my name was on his left rib. Meech had so many tattoos that I never even noticed it. But without speaking, I went in to kiss him again. I don't know what I did to get so lucky. But my mom used to always say, 'when God is getting ready to bless you, he's going to take you through a storm to humble you.'

The next day, after Queen's funeral, I went to her mother house and executed her the same way she had done mine. I knew I wasn't supposed to fight fire with fire. But seeing her beg gave me the satisfaction, I needed. Because in this family if you take on ours, we take on of yours.

After everything, we had been through life ended up perfect. A few of us still have scars to remind us of the pain. Then others just had the memories. This was one hell of a rollercoaster, but I enjoyed every bump on the ride.

"I love you, Paris Narcole!"

"I love you more, Jarcole!"